A Matter of Memory

A Matter of Memory

Lisa Sita

All our knowledge has its origins in our perceptions.

- Leonardo da Vinci

PART I

Chapter 1

June 15

When Luciano Benini left his house in Benvenuto one fine summer morning, he did not know that after returning later in the day, he would leave a second time, only this time he would not return.

Benvenuto was an ancient little town deep in the south of Italy, built on a mountain overlooking the Ionian Sea. Luciano and his wife Natalia had raised their son and daughter there on the modest, yet sufficient, earnings of the family grocery store. Although the small shop was well stocked, that particular morning Luciano would walk down the mountain to the large supermarket in Santa Chiara to purchase something special: the fresh mozzarella, silky and delicately textured, that was delivered there daily by a local cheesemaker. The mozzarella was to be a peace offering to Natalia, whom he had disgraced the night before by coming home drunk, finding Father Pietro there, and accidently vomiting on the priest's shoes. He hoped it would serve to placate her, as she had a particular fondness for it.

Natalia was downstairs in the kitchen when Luciano finished dressing and got ready to leave. He knew that if he ventured into the kitchen he would receive a frosty reception, if he received one at all, so he slipped down the stairs and left by the front door without so much as a word to his wife.

Outside, Luciano's spirits lifted in the warm sunshine so that his humiliation of the night before almost lost its sting. Strolling leisurely through the streets, across the piazza, and past his own store, he nodded and called out greetings to friends and neighbors.

Even at this early hour, the town was loud with activity because this day was the feast day of San Vito. San Vito was the town's patron saint, and all of Benvenuto was preparing to celebrate. On the main street, men on ladders hung strings of bulbs on covered stalls and across buildings to light at nightfall, and vendors busily set up tables that would sell everything from gelato and panini to clothing and religious statues. In a few hours there would be dancing, singing, and socializing, with loud holiday revelry echoing through the streets.

Luciano left the town behind and began the long walk to the shore. Halfway down the mountain, a car whizzing along the curved road slowed beside him.

Enzo the barber leaned out of the driver's side window. "What are you doing out here?" he asked.

"I'm going to the supermarket," said Luciano. "Where are you going?"

"Maggento, to pick up my nephew for the feast."

Luciano nodded an acknowledgement.

"Get in," said Enzo. I'll give you a ride to Santa Chiara."

"No, thanks. It's out of your way, and I need the exercise." Luciano patted his stomach, which was flat and did not appear to need exercise. In truth, Luciano still felt the effects of last night's wine and hoped the long walk in the fresh air would do him good.

"If you're sure . . ."

"I'd rather walk, really."

With a nod and a wave, Enzo continued on his way and Luciano continued on his until he reached Santa Chiara at the base of the mountain.

The supermarket in Santa Chiara was large, well lit, and modern. It sat on a street along the shoreline beside a stretch of beach. On market days local vendors set up stalls along the beach, but today it was quiet, with only a few people—tourists most likely, and a few locals who were not at home or working—splashing in the water or sitting in folding chairs and on blankets on the warm sand.

Luciano breathed in the clean sea air and lingered on the street for a moment, enjoying the calmness of the waves rippling along the shore, before entering the supermarket. After selecting a large mozzarella for Natalia, a bottle of Chianti, and a package of almond biscotti, he left the store with his purchases and headed towards the beach.

* * *

Natalia did not want to be angry on this day of all days, as it was a holy day, and she wanted to keep her baser emotions under control. But Mass was to begin at eleven and Luciano was nowhere to be found. She had heard the front door open and shut several hours earlier, and as their teenage daughter Liliana had still been asleep, Natalia knew it was her husband who had left the house. Now, at ten thirty, she and Liliana were dressed in their finest and ready to walk to the church without him.

"Maybe we should wait a few more minutes," said Liliana as they entered the foyer.

"You know we have to get there early or else the pews will be packed. I don't want to stand. And you know Father Pietro always begins Mass precisely on time."

"Maybe papa is still embarrassed from last night and doesn't want to face him."

"I'm sure he is embarrassed, but that's no excuse for keeping us waiting."

"He might meet us there."

Natalia frowned and opened the front door. "Let's hope so."

"You're still mad at him, aren't you?" asked Liliana as they wound through the streets, high heels clicking on the pavement.

"Liliana, just be quiet please."

The steps of Santa Maria degli Angeli were thick with parishioners flowing into the church through its massive wooden doors. Natalia and Liliana slipped into a pew at the back of the church and waited for Mass to begin. As it was a day of celebration, the church was crammed with the usual attendees, as well as those who came only on holy days and tourists enjoying the local traditions.

Liliana sat quietly flipping through the missalette and occasionally looking up to see if any of her friends had come in. Natalia looked over her shoulder every few minutes towards the door.

"Why do you keep doing that?" asked Liliana. "It's not going to make him come any sooner. If he shows up, he shows up."

"He belongs here with us. How does it look that we're here without your father?"

"Who cares how it looks? You're only getting yourself upset."

Natalia looked long at her daughter and shook her head. At sixteen, Liliana had more sense than most girls her age. "I suppose you have a point," she said grudgingly. Maybe she was overreacting. Luciano might well have a good reason for not being there.

Natalia sat up straight and looked ahead to the altar, noticing how lovely it looked with clusters of potted lilies and daffodils placed on the floor in front of it. When the first chords of the organ rang out and the congregation stood, Natalia turned her attention towards the processional coming up the aisle. She would not trouble herself with Luciano anymore.

* * *

The sun beaming through the stained-glass windows of Santa Maria degli Angeli shed mosaics of bright colors onto Eva Amadeo's long black hair and onto her lap. Eva sat at the end of a pew with her parents, Maria and Umberto, and her older brother Sandro. She wore her favorite dress, a simple print of yellow silk, and her best white lace shawl.

As Father Pietro gave his homily, Eva glanced around the church with a small twist of her head, hoping no one would notice. Normally, she enjoyed listening to Father Pietro, whose voice was always buoyant with enthusiasm, but today she was distracted. Alessandro Cento, the butcher's son with the bright brown eyes, was not among the worshippers. Alessandro worked as a waiter in Maggento and was most likely serving breakfast to some tourist right at that moment. Finding him absent from the Mass, Eva hoped her disappointment did not show on her face. She didn't like the idea of parading her vulnerability in front of her friends and neighbors. She was not a child anymore. She was a young woman of eighteen, and she had her pride.

Eva drew her attention back to the Mass. Alessandro, she was sure, would come to the feast in the evening.

* * *

When Luciano woke up lying on his side in the sand, the sun was high overhead. The bag from the supermarket and the wine bottle lay beside him. The bag still contained the mozzarella and a few biscotti, but the bottle was empty.

Luciano pulled himself into a sitting position, the same position he had started out in. After leaving the supermarket, he had settled himself on the beach to look out over the water while he ate the biscotti. They were sweet and crunchy, and he had only intended to take a few sips of the wine, just enough to wash down the crumbs. But the sun reflecting off the water mesmerized him so that he sipped without thinking until a calm warmth infused his body, and his thoughts wandered across the ocean. He mused over what it would be like to live somewhere out there, in America perhaps, or one of the Latin American countries, wondering if he would be a grocer there, or if another calling would await him, and if houses and land came cheaply or if a man had to struggle to make a living. After a while he became tired and struggled to keep his eyes open. The next thing he knew he had awakened with his cheek on the sand and a cramp in the arm he was lying on.

Luciano stood up slowly, still lightheaded from the wine. He stretched out his arm and brushed the sand off his clothes. He was not wearing a watch, but the sun told him it was past noon. Natalia, already upset with him from the night before, would be furious. He had missed Mass and had gone off without telling her where he was going or when he would be back. He couldn't even count on his peace offering to soften her, as it was most likely not enough to appease her for a double offense, and, even worse, it had been sitting out in the sun for several hours and would have lost its delicate flavor.

Luciano picked up the bag and the wine bottle, brought them over to a nearby trash can, and dumped them in. With a sigh of self-reproach and dread for what he would face when he got home, he crossed the street and began the long walk back up the mountain.

* * *

Eva walked leisurely with her mother among the canopied market stalls, pausing now and then to examine some item or talk to a neighbor. When they stopped to admire a gallery of hand-painted miniature landscapes displayed by an artist from a neighboring town, their attention was drawn to a stirring at the church steps. The saint's procession was about to begin.

Inside the church, volunteers had carefully and lovingly placed the nearly life-size statue of San Vito on its ornately carved litter festooned with colorful garlands. The saint had been a child of thirteen when he was martyred, and the statue reflected his youth with the painted face of a boy. Its plaster hand held a small cross, and it was dressed in the tunic of the Roman Empire into which Vito had been born—a white covering of loose cloth with a red cloak buttoned over one shoulder.

Those gathered on the church steps parted to make room for Father Pietro and his attendants, who were followed by San Vito supported on the shoulders of the town's strongest men and boys. To the vibrant music of a brass band, the statue bearers made their way down the steps and to the street, carefully balancing the heavy litter swaying with their movement. A woman walked behind them holding a pennant, an invitation to the faithful to pin donations of money to the cloth as the procession made its way through the streets.

Eva moved away from the artist's stall and positioned herself in front of a fruit stand to watch them pass. Absorbed in the pageantry, she did not notice Alessandro walk up beside her.

"Good afternoon, Eva," he said.

Eva smiled. So he had come after all.

"And how are you today?" he asked, looking over the selection of fruit.

"I'm well." She could think of nothing else to say as she watched Alessandro choose an apple from the display and pay for it.

"Would you like one?" he asked.

"No, thank you."

"Well, enjoy the day," he said with a smile and turned to go.

"Wait."

"Yes?"

"Maybe I'll see you later for the fireworks?"

"Maybe." He smiled and began to walk away.

"Alessandro," she called after him. "I'll be watching them from the steps of the church."

He grinned and waved, then strolled off into the crowd without looking back. He had a way of walking that radiated confidence, a flow of long strides that made Eva think of ocean currents. She watched him until he was out of sight.

Turning to look for her mother, Eva bumped into someone passing beside her. It was Natalia Benini, the grocer's wife. Natalia frowned.

"Excuse me," said Eva.

Natalia nodded and continued walking.

Eva knew Natalia didn't like her. Natalia didn't like the Amadeos generally, a fact she made no effort to disguise. Her dislike had its origin two years prior, when Sandro had politely refused an invitation from Natalia's daughter to accompany her to a local dance. Liliana was a nice girl, and pretty, too, but Sandro wanted to go to the dance with Gianna Gallo, and this perceived slight to her daughter caused Natalia to resent Sandro and, by extension, all Amadeos. Eva didn't care, her family didn't care, and it seemed Liliana didn't care, either, as she shortly afterwards turned her attention to another boy and lost all interest in Sandro.

Eva's mother came up beside her. "Have you seen

your father and your brother?"

"Papa was over by the church when I last saw him, and I haven't seen Sandro since Mass ended."

"I saw you talking to Natalia Benini. What did she have to say?"

"Nothing. I bumped into her, that's all.'

"And she didn't say anything?"

"No, she just scowled at me. That woman always looks so angry."

"I remember when we were girls, she never used to look like that. She grew into that expression."

"Why is that?"

"I don't know. Maybe her life just didn't turn out the way she had planned."

Eva shrugged. She hoped her own life, no matter how hard it might get, would never turn her sour like that.

* * *

Natalia wove through the crowd looking for Liliana and found her examining jewelry at one of the stalls. "I'm going home," she said. "Do you want to come home to have something to eat?"

"No, I'll get something here. You'll be back later, right?"

"I suppose. If you see your father, tell him I've been looking for him."

The joyous sounds of the feast followed Natalia as she left. She had been in a bad mood all morning, and as the day wore on and still Luciano had not shown up, her annoyance grew. It was a terrible habit of his to go off on his own with no explanation, a habit he had cultivated soon after the children were born. Perhaps if he hadn't disgraced her the night before she could be more forgiving, but he should have made more of an effort to be with his family on this public day. Bumping into Eva

Amadeo only made Natalia more irritated. Why didn't the girl pay attention to where she was going? Too caught up in paying attention to the butcher's son, most likely.

Natalia stepped into the foyer of her home and shut the door against the music of the band and the noise of the crowd coming from the center of town. She was about to go to the kitchen to prepare lunch for herself when the sound of running water upstairs stopped her. Someone was taking a shower, and there was only one person it could be because she had left Liliana behind at the feast.

Natalia went upstairs into her bedroom and waited. When Luciano came into the bedroom wearing a towel around his waist, he stopped short at the sight of her.

"I was about to go find you at the feast," he said. "I just needed to come home first to shower. I was sweaty."

Natalia pursed her lips. "Where have you been all day?"

"I went to Santa Chiara to buy that mozzarella you like."

"You went to Santa Chiara to buy the mozzarella I like. How long does it take to buy mozzarella?"

"I walked. You know it's a long walk down the mountain."

"I will ask again, how long does it take to buy mozzarella even when you walk to get it?"

"Natalia, please. I did it for you."

"For me?"

"Yes, for you. Why are you angry? Really, Natalia, sometimes you give me such a hard time for little things."

"Little things?"

"Will you stop repeating everything I say!"

"You have no respect, Luciano, no respect for me, and no consideration. You just do whatever you want without ever thinking of anyone else. What would it have taken to tell me that you were going to Santa Chiara and that you would be there most of the day? Instead, you leave me to guess what happened to you. You do this all the time and it's wrong!"

"I wanted it to be a surprise."

"Oh, it was a surprise, all right."

"I meant the mozzarella. I wanted to make up for embarrassing you last night."

"And you think you could do that with cheese?"

"I give up." Luciano yanked open a dresser drawer and began pulling clothes out. He unwrapped the towel, put on fresh underwear, and slipped into a pair of jeans under his wife's condemning glare.

As Luciano finished dressing, Natalia stormed out of the room and down the stairs.

Chapter 2

When night fell in Benvenuto, the streets glowed in the soft light of the stalls. The statue of San Vito, draped in twinkling lights, stood in front of the church on a platform erected especially for it. The brass band had stopped playing earlier in the day, and now a string orchestra made up of musicians from the surrounding towns entertained the crowd.

Eva sat on the church steps and waited for the announcement that the fireworks would soon begin. But when a loud whistling followed by a staccato of blasts sent the first explosion into the sky, Eva was not paying attention. She didn't look up at the colorful display sprinkling out over the rooftops of the town because Alessandro had not yet come to join her. As burst after burst of fireworks exploded above her, Eva's heart deflated more and more.

And then she saw him. He came around the corner, past a stall selling gelato, and right past the church steps, his arm around the waist of Anna, the doctor's daughter. He was saying something in her ear, and she laughed, turning her face from him, pretending she was not enjoying his attention. A sharp pain seared Eva's chest.

She pushed her way through the people on the steps and jostled through the crowd towards the end of the street, towards anywhere that was away from the sight of Alessandro, the butcher's son, and Anna, the doctor's daughter, entwined and giggling like fools.

* * *

Natalia watched the fireworks from the piazza. It was less crowded there, less noisy than on the main street. After she had left Luciano dressing in their bedroom, she had remained in the house for most of the afternoon and had set herself to cleaning—sweeping the floors, dusting the furniture, and doing the laundry—activities that required no thought and which always calmed her. When she later returned to the feast, neither she nor Liliana could find Luciano, and Natalia tried to enjoy the remainder of the celebration without him. From where she now sat on the rim of the central fountain, she could see the façade of the family grocery store, dark and shuttered, as it had been all day for the feast. She had hoped to see a light within, hoped that Luciano was inside so that she could go to him and talk, let him know she had not meant to be so harsh with him. He had, after all, tried to do something nice for her that day. Sometimes she regretted the quick-tempered outbursts she often lobbed at him. If only he would stop now and then to think things through before going off to do some hair-brained scheme, like drinking too much or wandering off to buy mozzarella on a feast day. Luciano never looked ahead to potential consequences.

The onlookers applauded as a loud series of bursts exploded in the sky, creating a sparkling display of outstretched angels' wings in blues, whites, and golds followed by the shimmering image of San Vito. Legend said that the adolescent Vito had driven an evil spirit out of the Emperor Diocletian's son, but instead of being grateful, the emperor had the Christian Vito thrown into a cauldron of molten lead when he refused to make a sacrifice to the Roman gods. Maybe Natalia had thrown Luciano into a cauldron of her own that day—a cauldron of molten anger—when she rebuked him. While she didn't consider Luciano anywhere close to a martyred saint, maybe she should have been grateful for the cheese.

* * *

As Eva pushed hurriedly through the crowd, she would not allow herself to cry. She would not give Alessandro and Anna that satisfaction, even though they couldn't see her and couldn't know they were the cause of her distress. She slowed her pace when she reached the piazza, where the throng of revelers was thinner, past Natalia Benini, who sat gazing up at the fireworks, and on through the town until the streets ended and she was in the countryside. She wandered for a while, absorbed in her unhappiness, then sat to rest on a wide, flat boulder by the edge of a ravine.

Eva looked out upon the night through the trees. A full white moon was cradled in a clear sky pierced by bright stars. The distance from the town softened the sounds of celebration and the noise of the fireworks, but it could not fade the picture in Eva's mind of how pretty Anna had looked and how much Alessandro had gushed over the girl's feigned indifference. A pain rose in Eva's throat; a surge of hot tears streamed over her cheeks and dropped onto the front of her dress. She pulled her shawl closer around her shoulders.

Startled by a rustle in the brush behind her, she turned abruptly to see who it was, when out of the darkness came Luciano Benini. He took an unsteady step forward, and Eva could see that he had been drinking. Not wishing to be caught with her heart exposed, Eva wiped her eyes and forced a smile. Dark and handsome, with deep blue eyes, Luciano reminded her of an American movie star, the kind who played the leading roles in the black-and-white movies of old Hollywood.

"What are you doing here?" he asked. "Have you had enough of the feast and people telling you what to do?"

His slurred words confused her. No one had told her what to do. She didn't answer.

Luciano staggered over to the rock, sat down beside her, sighed, and went quiet.

Eva did not understand why Luciano was there, out in the countryside instead of in town with his family. She had not seen him at the feast that day. Maybe he was hiding from his wife. It was widely known that Natalia made a habit of persecuting him, especially when she caught him praising other women, although no one in Benvenuto would ever accuse Luciano of being unfaithful. He was known, instead, for his practice of unhappily running off to seek refuge in his own company. Just a few weeks earlier Eva had seen him at the outdoor market in Santa Chiara standing on the beach and gazing out towards the sea, a creamy pink shell plucked from the shallow water nestled in his cupped hand. There seemed to be a longing in the way he stared into the distance, as if he wanted to flee across the waves in search of something better than Benvenuto. When she greeted him, he seemed at first to not recognize her, lost instead in a daydream. Then he smiled and told her how pretty she looked.

Now, as Eva sat beside him, rigid and uncomfortable in her misery, Luciano turned to her and, looking intently into her face, seemed to suddenly notice that she had been crying. She turned away, embarrassed.

"What's wrong?" he asked.

Eva shook her head in reply. She wished he would leave.

"You know," he continued, "I never meant to stay away so long. I just wanted to eat my breakfast."

Eva had no idea what he was talking about. She tried to tune him out as he blabbered on, offering explanations that made no sense to her: how he had bought the mozzarella for Natalia and had meant to spend no more than an hour in Santa Chiara, how it had been so easy to finish the bottle of Chianti once it was opened, and how he had fallen asleep on the beach, realizing when he awoke that he had missed Mass, and how Natalia was furious with him, so what could he do but go off to his closed grocery shop to be by himself and drink even more wine in the back room to dull the edge of his wife's cutting words, and how he then left the shop to get some fresh air and found his way here to the place where Eva sat.

"Luciano," she said, "please, I just want to be alone."

His expression turned into one of sad empathy. "Did someone hurt you?"

Eva suspected that what he did next was meant as a kindness, an offer to lean on another wounded human for comfort, but Eva did not want his sympathy. Luciano lifted his arm to place around her shoulder. Although she didn't fear him, his drunkenness repulsed her, so when his arm came around to embrace her, she pushed him away. Her shawl came loose in his hand as he stumbled to get up off the rock. Unsteady on his feet and still clutching the shawl, he grabbed the trunk of a chestnut tree and caught his foot in an exposed root. Eva lunged forward to help him when he slipped and tumbled into the ravine. He made hardly a sound as he fell, only the *swoosh* of his clothing catching on the vegetation as he slid down.

Eva clung to the chestnut tree and leaned out over the ravine. In the shadows below, Luciano's body lay motionless on the ground. Her shawl, cast from his hand, glowed like luminescent white froth on the undergrowth.

For a few moments Eva could not move. She stared, numb with horror, into the void at Luciano's rigid body. Then, loosening her arms from around the tree, she eased herself onto the boulder, shaking now and unable to look down again. Taking deep breaths, she waited for the shaking to subside. When it didn't, she forced herself to get up and make her way back to the road. In the distance, the string orchestra was still playing as she ran back to town.

* * *

Luciano awakened in the moonlit countryside at the bottom of the ravine, his body ablaze with pain. He lay on his back, his neck twisted, his cheek resting in a clump of overgrown grass and stray twigs, with an unbearable throbbing at the back of his head. When he tried to pull himself up, every bone and muscle pulsated in agony. He fell back again against the uneven ground, still drunk, and he wasn't sure if it was the drink or the pain that caused his eyes to go in and out of focus as he tried to orient himself. For a moment, Luciano couldn't remember anything, but as he stared up into the trees, he hazily recalled sitting with Eva Amadeo on a boulder high above him. He could not remember what they had talked about, but he knew he had attempted to comfort her. The last thing he remembered was the frightful lurch of his stomach as he fell.

Wincing, Luciano turned slowly to look up at the boulder. No one was there. Somewhere far off an orchestra was playing a tarantella. With great effort he pulled himself into a sitting position and waited for the throbbing in his head to subside. He didn't know how long he had been unconscious. His shirt was torn, and his exposed hands and arms were scratched. Touching his face, he flinched—a cut ran from his cheek to his temple.

A few feet away lay a wide fallen branch, darkened with blood, and a woman's shawl, bloodied and streaked with dirt, beside it. Luciano placed his hand to the back of his head and felt a wet stickiness there. He tried to connect the shawl with the blood, *his* blood. Or was it? Had he done something to Eva Amadeo? Why was her shawl in the ravine with him? He dragged himself to the branch and reached for the shawl. For several minutes he stared at it clutched in his hand, his vision blurred, before keeling over and throwing up into the bushes.

* * *

The house was empty and unlit when Eva arrived home. Her nerves on fire, she made her way to the living room, zombie-like, without turning on any lights, lowered herself onto the sofa, and sat stiffly in the dark, waiting for her parents and brother to return from the feast. When the key in the front door finally turned, she didn't move.

Her mother jumped, startled, when she switched on the light and found Eva sitting there. "What's going on?" she asked. "What's wrong?"

Eva's father and brother entered the room behind her mother.

"Something's happened," said Eva. Seeing the fear in all their faces, she quickly described in a trembling voice her encounter with Luciano Benini and how she had pushed him to his death in the dark of night.

Her father frowned. "Don't be ridiculous," he said. "What makes you think he's dead? He tripped, that's all. It wasn't your fault."

"He wasn't moving, papa."

"How do you know that?" her mother asked. "How could you see anything in the dark?"

"There was no movement. I could see that much."

"You said he'd been drinking," said Sandro. "He

probably passed out."

"Are none of you listening to me!" she shouted. He fell down the side of the mountain."

"He slid down a ravine," said her father. "I'm sure when he wakes up, he'll go right back home."

"No!" Eva cried, wringing her hands. "No. You don't understand. You didn't see him lying there."

"Calm down," said her mother. "You've had a bad fright, that's all. Maybe you should go to bed, get some rest."

Eva shot up from the sofa and began pacing the room. "Rest!" she said. "You think I can rest after this?"

Eva's father looked long and hard at her. He headed towards the door.

"Where are you going, papa?" asked Sandro.

"To find him."

"Umberto," cried his wife, "it's late. This is not a good idea."

"You see the state she's in. She won't get any rest until this is straightened out."

"I'll go with you," said Sandro.

"I'm going, too," said Eva.

"Eva, you stay right here," said her mother. "This is foolish, looking for a man passed out drunk in the dark."

"Come along, Eva," said her father. "Maria, she has to see for herself. Sandro, you stay with your mother."

After grabbing a flashlight from the kitchen, Umberto and Eva left the house and hurried through town. Now that the feast had ended, the streets were quieter, with only a few remnants left of the crowd still lingering in the piazza and in the cafes that remained open for the tourists.

"There," said Eva, pointing, when they reached the place where Eva had sat that night.

Umberto stepped onto the boulder and looked down into the ravine.

"Do you see him, papa?"

Supporting his weight on the chestnut tree beside the boulder, he turned his flashlight downwards and scanned the area.

Eva shuddered. "Be careful, papa. That's the same tree where his foot got caught."

"Stay here. I'm going down."

"I'm coming down with you."

"I said stay here!"

As her father climbed slowly into the ravine, Eva watched his every step, silently praying he wouldn't fall. After what seemed like hours, he came back up, disheveled by the climb, her lace shawl wrapped around his wrist. With one last pull on the surrounding vegetation and with the help of Eva pulling on his arm, Umberto heaved himself up onto the boulder.

"Oh, my God," said Eva at seeing the shawl "there's blood on it! Was he there? Is he bleeding?"

Breathing heavily from the climb, Umberto put his hand out to silence his daughter. "No," he said. "He's not there."

"But there's blood down there! There's blood on my shawl."

Umberto nodded, unwrapping the shawl from his wrist.

Eva wrung her hands. "Get that away from me. I don't want it now."

"Eva, there's no one down there, dead or otherwise. Calm down."

"But there's blood. Maybe he crawled off and died somewhere else."

"The blood was on a branch lying on the ground. He probably hit his head on it. He's not there, Eva. I'm sure he'll turn up at his house if he's not there already. Now come on, let's go home. It's been a long day, and I know your mother is worried about us."

"Throw that away, first," she said, pointing to the

shawl. "I don't want to see it."

"We'll throw it away at home."

Eva took her father's arm and together they walked slowly back to the house, Eva nursing a weak hope that Luciano was still alive.

Chapter 3

June 16

When dawn broke, Luciano found himself lying on the ground, his shirt ripped and soiled, his arms and hands scraped and caked with dried blood. He remembered he had fallen, lost consciousness, awakened, and vomited. But why was he still lying in underbrush in the countryside instead of at home? Closing his eyes against the raging pain at the back of his head, he tried to piece together the details of the previous night and had a foggy recollection of stumbling in the dark through trees and brush, disoriented and confused. He must have fallen unconscious again or just fallen asleep—he wasn't sure— but now he was awake and had to get home. Natalia would be livid by now.

The sound of rapidly passing vehicles told Luciano he was close to the coastal road. He pulled himself up on unsteady feet, swayed a little, and stumbled forward out of the trees. In the distance, the sky cast a pink glow over a calm sea. Luciano looked down the road and saw the buildings of Santa Chiara. He knew he was somewhere between Santa Chiara and Lauri, the next seaside town over. The road was quiet at this hour, with almost no traffic. Suddenly feeling nauseous, he sat down on the ground and put his head between his knees.

A delivery truck pulled up alongside him and stopped. Luciano looked up to see a young stocky man come around from the driver's side and stoop down next to him.

"Are you all right?" the young man asked.

Luciano nodded.

"Well, you certainly don't look all right. You look like you need a hospital."

Luciano waved his hand in dismissal, but the wave was weak and the man persistent.

"My name is Marco," he said, helping Luciano up off the ground. "There's a hospital in Lauri. I'm going that way anyway, so come on."

Luciano did not resist as Marco shuffled him over to the truck and into the passenger side of the cab. Once they were both inside, Marco pulled a cloth from the glove compartment and doused it with water from a plastic bottle on the dashboard. "For the blood," he said, handing it to Luciano.

Luciano gently patted the back of his head with the cloth. The water felt cool and soothing. The cloth turned red.

Marco pulled the truck onto the road and quickly picked up speed. He glanced at Luciano, who remained quiet. "What's your name?" he asked.

"Luciano."

"Luciano, you're in bad shape."

"Yes."

"What happened to you?"

"I'd rather not talk about it."

"Are you in some kind of trouble?"

"Look," said Luciano, weary and not in the mood to answer questions, "I appreciate that you stopped and that you're giving me this ride, but I really just want to rest."

Marco nodded and continued to drive without another word.

* * *

A nightmare roused Natalia from her bed in the early morning after a fitful sleep. She couldn't remember what it was, but its wispy tendrils left a pall hanging over her for several long moments as she lay staring up at the shadowy ceiling. When the veil between dream and reality had burned away, she turned on her side and was met with a disturbing sight—her husband's side of the bed had not been slept in.

Natalia got out of bed and quietly passed the half-open door of the bathroom. The light was off, and no one was inside. Beside the bathroom was her son Fabiano's room. Fabiano was away at university, studying art history in Florence, and the room was not being used. She opened the door. The room was exactly as Fabiano had left it, the furniture all in its place, including his bed, neatly made. Luciano was not there.

Natalia passed Liliana's closed bedroom door and went downstairs. Passing quickly through the kitchen, dining room, and living room and finding no Luciano, she went out the back door and into the yard. Luciano was not there, either. This was not like him, and she began to worry. For all his wanderings, Luciano always came home, never letting a night pass without sleeping in his own bed.

Her heart tumbling in her chest, Natalia went back into the house and phoned the grocery store. Maybe Luciano had drunk too much at the feast and spent the night at the store rather than come home and face her. It would have been an unusual move for him, but she was desperate for an explanation. Tapping her foot on the tile floor, she listened impatiently to the ringing as she waited for him to answer. When the ringing stopped and her own voice asked the caller to please leave a message, Natalia hung up.

After a moment's hesitation, she went upstairs to dress. She had to find Luciano, and she would start by asking her neighbors if anyone had seen him.

As she was leaving her room, Liliana came out into the hallway. "What's going on?" she asked. "Why are you already dressed so early in the morning?"

Natalia didn't want to alarm her daughter. She didn't know what to say.

"Mama, why do you have that strange look on your face?"

"I don't have a strange look. I'm just going out for a walk."

"You're not telling me the truth, are you?"

Natalia took a deep breath and bit her lip. "I have to go look for your father."

"What do you mean 'look for him'? Didn't he go to the store?"

"I don't know where he is. He didn't come home last night."

Liliana looked stricken.

"Don't worry," said Natalia, "I'm sure he has a good reason. I'll be back soon."

"I'll go with you."

"No, you wait here in case he comes back."

Natalia hurried down the stairs and out of the house.

* * *

The lights in the emergency room were bright, and the pain in Luciano's head was made worse by the cacophony of hospital noises. The young truck driver, after seeing Luciano safely admitted to the emergency room, had left, and now Luciano sat in a plastic chair, bruised and exhausted, waiting for a doctor to see him.

It could be a long wait, and the chair was

uncomfortable. Despite the pain in his muscles and joints, he was able to move freely, if slowly, so he was sure none of his bones were broken. Maybe he didn't need to be here. Maybe all he needed was a long, hot bath and some rest.

Luciano wondered how bad his face looked. None of the other patients showed any horror at his appearance or seemed to take any notice of him at all; they had their own troubles to attend to. What Luciano needed was a mirror. Looking around, he saw a washroom near the emergency room entrance not far from where he sat. He tried to ignore the aches in his limbs as he carefully lifted himself out of the chair and wearily shuffled to it.

The washroom was a single room and unoccupied. Luciano saw his reflection in the mirror above the sink as soon as he stepped in. He had expected to see two black eyes and a swollen face, but besides the gash on his cheek and a small purple discoloration on his chin, he had only a few minor cuts and scratches. Touching the back of his head where he had struck the fallen branch, he found that the wound there, like the cuts on his face and arms, had crusted over.

Luciano leaned over the sink and doused his face and hair with water. He ran his arms under the flow to wash away the caked blood on his scrapes and scratches. With a soaked towel, he did his best to clean off the dirt from his clothes. As he washed, the thought of Eva's bloodstained shawl terrified him. Although his mind was still sluggish and his recollections muddled, he remembered Eva pushing him away. Had he then pushed *her* without meaning to, and had she fallen on the rock and hit her head? Had he unintentionally pulled her into the ravine with him? She had not been beside him when he had first awakened, but he didn't know how long he had been unconscious. Maybe she had crawled away from him and was now lying hurt somewhere in the woods, or even dead? But surely someone from Benvenuto—her parents most likely—would have gone out looking for her. And if she were not hurt, she would certainly have gone back to town and told someone that Luciano Benini was lying unconscious at the bottom of a ravine. Yet the night had been quiet. As far as he could tell, no one had gone out looking for either of them.

Leaning on the washroom sink, his haggard and frustrated face staring back at him from the mirror, Luciano knew only one thing: he could not risk going home until he was sure he had not done anything terrible—anything criminal—to Eva Amadeo.

He hurried from the washroom and left the hospital as quickly as his injured body would allow. Once on the street, he felt for his wallet. Despite the fall, and fortunately for the slim fit of his jeans, the wallet had remained tucked into his back pocket. He opened it and counted the money inside, more than enough to buy a train ticket out of the area. He needed time to think.

* * *

Natalia had spent almost two hours ringing her neighbors' doorbells in a near panic, asking if anyone had seen her husband. A few had seen him at the feast, they said, but only in passing. They shrugged and tried not to look her in the eye because they knew Luciano could be counted on to vanish for hours at a time, coming home at odd hours, smelling of too much wine and grumbling because the pasta she had prepared had lumped into a soft, sticky mass the color of a drowned man three days in the water. By the time she came to the barber shop, where Enzo was just opening for the day, Natalia struggled to hold back tears.

"I saw him yesterday morning," said Enzo. "He was walking down the mountain to Santa Chiara. I offered him a ride, but he refused."

"And you didn't see him after that? You didn't see him last night or this morning?"

Enzo shook his head, his face solemn. "I'm sorry, no."

Natalia left the barber shop in a fit of anxiety and hurried towards the grocery store. Maybe Luciano had been in a deep sleep when she had phoned the shop earlier and hadn't heard the ringing. When she reached the store and saw that it was closed, she let herself in and passed through to the storeroom at the back, hoping to find Luciano asleep on the floor. Seeing that he was not there, and with her hope extinguished, Natalia closed the shop and walked across town towards the Benvenuto police station.

* * *

It was early evening when Luciano arrived in Rome, a location far enough from Benvenuto that he could safely move about without detection. First, he had to purchase a change of clothes and some basic toiletries to get him through the next couple of days. He knew he looked rough, and the stares he had gotten from the other passengers when he boarded the train in Lauri, the way the conductor had frowned at him when he handed over his ticket, had made him uncomfortable.

Walking the streets amid the onslaught of traffic and pedestrians, Luciano recalled the last time he had been to Rome. It was with Natalia many years earlier when the children were young. They had treated themselves to a weekend away, just the two of them, leaving Liliana and Fabiano in the care of Natalia's uncle Maurizio. They had stayed in a luxury hotel just blocks from the Tiber, taking long evening walks along the river in the glow of the setting sun. The money Luciano now had in his wallet would not cover a room in a hotel like that, and he dared not use his credit card for fear of being traced should the police be looking for him. There were far less expensive lodgings in the city, so he looked for one of the many tourist kiosks on the street. Finding one, he browsed the brochures for the cheapest accommodation close to where he was standing and chose a convent guest house, the Casa di Santa Rosalia.

The salesgirl at one of the clothes shops told Luciano where he could find the guest house, and after making his purchases, he walked to the Casa and rang the bell, a plastic bag in each hand. He waited nervously until the heavy, wide door was opened by a small, smiling sister. She showed no sign of surprise or disdain at his appearance.

"May I help you?" she asked.

"Yes, I need a room please."

The sister admitted him into a neat, bright foyer and gestured towards the reception desk. Slipping behind the desk, she typed something into a computer and asked him his name. Luciano hesitated. The first name that came to him was Bruno—brown—because that was how he felt, dull and muted. Bruno Fiorentino. He had known a boy in school named Fiorentino. It was a random thought.

"How long will you be staying with us?"

"I'm not sure. A few days maybe."

"I will need your card information," said the sister.

Luciano looked at the list of room prices and the required deposit posted on a small sign beside the computer. "I have cash," he said, placing his bags on the floor and taking out his wallet.

The sister watched him pull out his money and carefully count it before handing it to her. He noticed she was taking in his appearance.

"*Signore*," she said, "some of our sisters are handy with a needle. We can sew the tears in your shirt if you like. No charge."

Luciano smiled, his eyes downcast. "Thank you, sister. That won't be necessary."

"May I have your address?"

Luciano looked away and smiled nervously. "I don't have one right now."

"I see. Where was your last place of residence?"

"Naples," he lied, and suddenly a flood of deception came out of his mouth. It came from some deep, desperate part of himself, and he was ashamed that he could not stop the words from flowing. "I was a factory worker there, in a shoe factory, but the business was not doing well so the boss let me go. I'm here in Rome looking for work."

The sister nodded thoughtfully as she handed him his key. "Your room is down the corridor on the left. There's a shared bathroom two doors down. And there's food in the refectory down the hall if you're hungry."

He thanked her, grateful that the ordeal of checking in under a false name was over. Although he had his shortcomings, lying was not one of them. He had always found it difficult.

Luciano's room was sparse but comfortable, with a single bed and plain pinewood furniture—a clothes cupboard, a nightstand with a lamp, and a small desk with a chair. A set of double windows looked out onto a quiet side street bathed in the glow of the early evening sun. At the foot of the bed lay a fresh towel, neatly folded. Luciano grabbed it and, taking both plastic bags with him, left the room to take a long shower. When he returned, clean and with a fresh change of clothes, he lay down on the bed.

For the first time that day, Luciano began to relax. The rumbling of his stomach reminded him that he had not eaten since the day before. Soon he would go down to the refectory, but now he needed to clear his mind and figure out his next move. He knew that Natalia would be furious, not to mention fiercely worried, yet he couldn't risk phoning her. If he had done something to Eva Amadeo, if the police came to their house and questioned Natalia, it was best that she knew nothing. And what would he say to her anyway? Thanks to his drunkenness at the time, he wasn't sure what had happened up on that rock. How could he admit that to Natalia? Even after all these years of marriage, he often did not know the best way to approach her. She could be calm and forgiving one minute, and hard and unyielding the next. But what family did not have their share of troubles? What man was without flaws? His way of coping whenever he upset Natalia was to become silent and morose and to find refuge outside of his house. He would close the shop at those times, a move that further incensed Natalia, but he always ignored her. It was his shop, he told her, to which she replied that his shop provided the livelihood for their family so that closing it meant losing money and pulling bread from their collective mouths.

A knock on his door pulled Luciano's attention from his troubles. It was the sister who had admitted him earlier.

"*Signore*, if you like, I can speak with Sister Michela, who is in charge of this guest house. She may give permission for you to do some work for us in lieu of payment for your room and meals until you find another job. We've done this occasionally in the past."

Luciano thought for a moment. "What kind of work?"

"Odd jobs. Cleaning, small repairs, helping the gardener with some of the heavier work on the grounds. That sort of thing."

"That's very kind of you, sister."

"Shall I speak to Sister Michela?"

Luciano nodded. Working at the Casa would allow him more time—time to think, time to keep an eye on the news, time to decide what to do. "Thank you, sister. Yes."

Chapter 4

June 19

Eva was awake in bed when Sandro knocked on her door. "Mama and papa want you downstairs. They're in the kitchen."

"They both want me? Why?

Sandro shook his head. "I don't know, but they look serious."

Sandro withdrew, and Eva got out of bed. They were probably going to force her to eat something or tell her that she needed to see a doctor. Since pushing Luciano into the ravine, she had been unable to keep down the few meager meals her mother forced her to eat, and her restless sleep had been plagued with nightmares. The past few days had been one long nightmare in itself. The police had been going from house to house asking questions. Eva's parents lied to them, saying they knew nothing. Some of the townspeople had searched for Luciano on their own, poking into all the nooks and crannies of the town, scouring the countryside on foot and in cars. Natalia had called her son home from Florence to assist, but no one could find Luciano. So the son returned to his university, Natalia waited for the authorities to locate her husband, and Eva remained hidden away at home, her nerves in a shambles.

Her parents were sitting at the table when she walked into the kitchen, their faces grim. The aroma of fresh coffee, normally a welcome fragrance, caused Eva's empty stomach to lurch.

"Sit down," said her mother.

Eva sat and looked expectantly from one parent to the other.

"I've called my sister in New York," said Maria. "Your father and I think it's best if you stay with her and your uncle for a while."

Eva looked at her mother in disbelief. "You want to send me away?"

"Only for a short while."

"Why? For how long?" Eva's head swirled with confusion. She had never been away from home, and now her parents wanted to send her across the ocean.

"A few months maybe, that's all."

"Months? You think the police will be back, don't you? You think they will arrest me."

"Absolutely not," said her father. "You haven't done anything wrong. But you're suffering, and you need some distance, some time away from here to recuperate."

"I'm not sick, papa. I don't need to recuperate."

"Your mother and I think it's best."

Eva shook her head vigorously. "Well, I don't. I won't go. I hardly know these people. The last time they came here I was a baby."

"They'll take good care of you," said her mother, "and their daughter Stella is only two years younger than you. She speaks Italian. You'll have someone your own age there to spend time with."

"No! I don't want to leave. I want to be here with you."

"Eva." Umberto's tone was firm. "We're not going to sit here and watch you waste away. You're going, and that's the end of it."

Eva's chest tightened and her cheeks flushed. The air in the house turned thick and suffocating. She needed to get away. Before either Maria or Umberto could do anything, she rose and ran out of the kitchen, out of the house.

As she hurried through the town, Eva took no notice of anyone around her. Most of the shops had already opened and the main street stirred with people. She rushed past them all. When she reached the piazza, she pulled herself up onto the rim of the fountain to catch her breath. In the distance, the roof of Santa Maria degli Angeli was white against the bright blue sky, its bell tower pointing like a finger to heaven. Eva thought how cruel it was that she had begun her day so happily at that very place just a few days before. Since then, through the turmoil of her emotions, she had wrestled with the idea of going to confession, to unburden herself and ask for God's forgiveness. She trusted Father Pietro, but even if she had not, she knew he was bound by the Seal of Confession never to reveal what she said. Yet repentance meant nothing without atonement, and she knew he would advise her to go to the police. The thought of doing that, of admitting she had pushed Luciano to what was likely his death, terrified her.

Eva clutched the rim of the fountain, steadying herself as she leaned over and focused on the cobblestones beneath her. She took deep breaths, her stomach churning. While she feared going to the police, banishment to America would be just another kind of prison, an indefinite separation from her family and friends, from all she knew and loved. It offered nothing less than life in a dreadful, lonely, far-away cell of her own making.

If Luciano really were dead, his end would have been the result of an accident, not a deliberate, calculated act.

Whatever evidence the police uncovered would prove that. It had to. She had no motive to harm Luciano, no past troubles with him. In fact, other than shopping in his grocery store and seeing him about town as she saw everyone else in Benvenuto, she had little to do with him, so how could she be charged?

Eva looked around the piazza with an aching heart. The sunlight was heating up the wide-open space. It flowed over the cobblestones and across the iron benches. A few people walked through, nodding to her in greeting. This was not a place she could willingly leave—this piazza, this town, the vibrant humanity of her neighbors living in these curving streets, people she had known since birth.

Eva took one last deep breath, hopped down from the fountain's rim, and left the piazza, walking briskly in the direction of the police station. Whatever the consequences, she would face them. She began to count silently, a distraction to take her mind off what she was about to do, when a strong hand grabbed her arm from behind. Startled, she swung around to find her father. In the moment before he spoke, before he told her to come home, Eva saw him again climbing up from the ravine on the night of the feast, disheveled and sweaty, her soiled shawl wrapped around his wrist. She suddenly realized why he had taken the shawl home that night instead of leaving it where he had found it, why he had taken it into the backyard and burned it. Without protest, she let him lead her back home.

* * *

While emptying trash in the refectory and thinking how, after three days in Rome, no one had come to arrest him, Luciano was summoned to Sister Michela's office. When one of the sisters came to tell him, he nodded and smiled, hoping to hide his apprehension. Sister Michela had agreed to let Luciano work temporarily at the guest house, and now that she wanted to meet with him, he was sure she had found him out. Since arriving, he had been diligently checking the news for any notice of his disappearance or of any criminal assault connected to him. Still, he was sure Sister Michela had discovered that he was a fraud with a fictitious name, and that she would demand answers.

Luciano washed his hands in the refectory's kitchen, straightened his clothes, and slowly walked upstairs to the large, paneled room that was Sister Michela's office. When he knocked gently on the open door, Sister Michela looked up from her papers and smiled. It was a pleasant smile, in a pleasant, full face, and a pang of guilt ran through him. How could he deceive these people who had treated him so kindly?

Sister Michela remained seated as Luciano entered the room. "Please, sit down," she said.

He sat in a leather armchair in front of a big mahogany desk where the sister's hands lay folded on the surface.

"Are you enjoying your stay here?"

He nodded. "Very much, yes."

Sister Michela smiled again. The wrinkles around her mouth and eyes softened, her face relaxing into an expression of sublime gentleness. She was a calm woman, embodying a serenity that could only come from a certainty that her life's work had meaning. Luciano envied her at that moment.

"I've been noticing you, Bruno, and I've been wondering if everything is okay. I ask because you seem a bit distracted at times. Even a little nervous."

Luciano coughed. "Everything is fine, sister. I'm fine."

"Perhaps it's the stress of losing your job."

"Please, sister, don't trouble yourself with me."

"Why do you consider it a trouble?"

"Well, I'm sure you're very busy, and to take time out of your work to concern yourself with me . . ."

"My work is to make sure everything runs smoothly in this guest house, and that includes making sure our staff as well as our visitors are happy. I realize you've only been here a few days, but have you had any success in finding permanent work?"

"Not yet, but I hope to find a job soon."

"I don't mean to pressure you. You're welcome to stay here until you do. However . . ."

"Yes?" Luciano shifted in his chair.

"You haven't really told us much about yourself."

At these words, a weight descended on him. Did she know something? Had someone from Benvenuto come looking for him?

The sister waited for a response.

Luciano lowered his eyes. "There's not much to tell. At least, nothing more than you already know. As I've explained, I used to work in a factory in Naples and lost my job."

"Are you sure?"

Luciano let out a small, humorless laugh. "What do you mean, sister?"

Sister Michela leaned forward in her chair and stared intently at him before answering. "I've been doing some research," she said, "and I've found no record of a Bruno Fiorentino who was let go from a shoe factory in Naples."

Luciano's face burned. Did this woman contact every shoe factory in Naples?

"Are you hiding from something, Bruno? Or someone?"

He shook his head, unable to speak.

"Will you at least tell me your real name?"

Luciano's chest tightened. So she did know something. "I can't," he said.

"Why not?"

He took a deep breath while Sister Michela waited patiently. "There was an accident," he said, "an injury to my head. I don't remember much."

Sister Michela retained her sense of calm while staring steadily at Luciano with skeptical yet compassionate eyes. "Are you saying you don't know who you are?"

Luciano wanted to trust her. She was a woman of God, after all. Instead, he lied to her again. "That's right."

"Then we must find your family. And you must see a doctor."

"No," he said quickly, getting up from his chair. "I will leave. You've been very generous, and I appreciate what you've done for me, but I'll be fine."

Sister Michela put her hand up. "Just a minute, Bruno." Luciano remained standing while she continued. "You may keep your job here until you find something else, and you may keep your room, but you must also allow us to make inquiries about you and try to locate your family."

Luciano thought for a moment and then nodded. He didn't know if Sister Michela actually believed him, or if she was just going along with his deception for reasons of her own, but he would allow her to make her inquiries if it meant he could stay at the Casa a little while longer. He knew he would have to go back to Benvenuto and face any consequences that might be waiting for him there. He was a man, after all, and men had to be men, even in the toughest of times. Yet, exhausted by the physical, emotional, and mental battering he had endured since his fall, he was not quite ready to return home. It was peaceful at the Casa, even with the coming and going of the guests, and Luciano found some relief in the rhythm of his work, in the kindness of the sisters, and in the tranquility of the garden these past three nights when everyone had gone to bed and he sat there alone in the fragrant stillness under a starry sky.

Luciano thanked Sister Michela and went back to his work. He no longer worried that she would discover who Bruno Fiorentino really was. By the time she did—*if* she did—Luciano Benini would be gone.

PART II

Chapter 5

May 9

As she drove the rental car up the mountain road towards Benvenuto, Eva Amadeo breathed in the fresh air flowing through the car's open windows. Far below the mountain, the sea rippled in azure wavelets against a cloudless sky, serene and indifferent.

It had been fifteen years since Eva had last seen Benvenuto. Images of her past came back in a bittersweet rush: memories of baking bread with her mother in their big bright kitchen, walking to school with her brother, the sound of the church bell ringing through the streets on Sunday mornings, and the loud, colorful knots of people strolling through the piazza every evening.

"It's magnificent!" said Stella for what seemed the hundredth time. Stella had never before witnessed the beauty of the southern Italian landscape.

"I can't look. I have to watch the road." From the corner of her eye, Eva saw her cousin lean out of the window.

"Why don't they put up guard rails?" asked Stella, craning her neck to see where the narrow winding road dropped off to the abyss below. "This is dangerous."

"Get your head in." With one arm outstretched, the other on the steering wheel, Eva yanked at Stella's brown ponytail until Stella settled back into the passenger seat.

"I can't believe it took you this long to come back here. If it weren't for Sandro's wedding, you'd still be making up excuses—don't have the money now, can't get off from work, not the right time of the year . . ." Stella prattled on.

No, Eva would not miss her brother's wedding. It took Sandro's engagement to Gianna—her brother's happiness—to bring her home.

"Oh, wow!" said Stella as they rounded a curve in the road and the squat buildings of the town, with their tawny-colored walls and red tiled roofs, appeared in stark relief against the deep blue sky. As they entered Benvenuto, Eva remained quiet while Stella yelped excitedly about how quaint and lovely everything was— the ancient walls and narrow streets, the balconies, the small shops and cafes—everything looking as if they were driving through a picture postcard.

It was Monday, and the town had shifted from its leisurely Sunday pace to its daily workday rhythm. They passed shops with doors open to the warm sunshine framing the people moving about inside. Women hung laundry out to dry on balconies while old men dug the soil in their gardens or sat in chairs in the shade playing cards. They stopped to stare as Eva and Stella passed. Stella was a stranger to them, but they recognized Eva and returned the smiles and waves she offered. Her arrival would be no surprise to the people of Benvenuto, where everyone knew the business of everyone else. Sandro Amadeo was getting married, and his sister was due to attend the wedding—this, she was sure, everyone knew weeks before her arrival.

It was not until they drove past the house where Natalia and Liliana Benini lived that Eva's smile faded and her stomach clenched. Eva had never entirely forgiven herself for what she had done to Luciano Benini out in the countryside all those years ago. What made matters worse was Natalia's conviction that Luciano was gone because of Eva, that Eva had seduced him into following her to America. Although it was a bizarre and false accusation, Eva did feel responsible for Natalia's loss, and she dreaded seeing her. While she could have taken a detour and avoided the house, she knew that running into Natalia was inevitable in a town as small as Benvenuto. Better to get it over with.

But the Benini house was shut up tight as a tomb. It was flush with the street, its front door opening onto the cobblestones. No one was on the small balcony above the door or at any of the front windows.

Stella seemed to notice the change in Eva's demeanor. "Something wrong?" she asked.

"No, of course not." Eva smiled. In all the years they had lived together, she had never told Stella why her parents had sent her to New York, only that she was there for a long vacation. Neither Eva nor her parents could have known at the time that Eva would choose to remain there.

Turning at the end of the street, they continued past the school Eva had attended as a child, past the Church of Santa Maria degli Angeli, and on to a wider street that led up a hill to her family's home.

The house was a large two-story structure with a balcony running the length of its upper floor. Rose bushes grew beneath the downstairs windows and a large cypress tree dominated the front yard. Beside the driveway, a stone pathway led to the front door.

As soon as Eva drove up, her mother ran outside and pulled Eva out of the car and into a crushing hug. Her father hurried after, with Sandro and his soon-to-be wife Gianna following behind. After delivering a barrage of kisses, Eva's mother released her and went for Stella, who laughed as she was swept into her aunt's embrace. Then Eva's father, his eyes wet, grabbed Eva in a tight hug and held her there, while Stella hugged Sandro and Gianna.

"Come," said Eva's mother, hooking one arm into Eva's and the other into Stella's as she led them towards the house. "You must eat something."

"We ate on the plane, mama."

Her mother frowned. "That's not real food, Eva. Stella, what can I make you? In America you eat a lot for breakfast, no? I have fresh eggs. I can make you a frittata and I have prosciutto and cheese and fruit and—

"Mama, it's too early for all that food."

"You need to eat something."

"Maria," Eva's father interjected with outstretched hands, "let them rest first. They just got here."

"Umberto, please. Get the suitcases and bring them upstairs. I'll take care of the girls. Sandro, help your father."

With a deep exhale, Eva's father shook his head and turned to get the suitcases, followed by a smiling Sandro, while the women walked into the house.

* * *

Natalia Benini, stocking a shelf in her grocery store on a street off the piazza, had counted the inventory of mineral water three times and each time had come up with a different number of bottles. Cursing under her breath, she began again.

Her daughter sat behind the counter flipping through a magazine. She got up and came over to where Natalia was working. "I'll do it," said Liliana.

"I can do it myself."

"It doesn't look like it."

Natalia pursed her lips and nodded for Liliana to go back behind the counter.

"They say she's going to be here for two weeks," said Liliana. "If you keep letting it bother you, you're going to be miserable."

Natalia stopped counting. "What do you suggest I do then?"

"Stop thinking about it."

"I can't stop thinking about it. And I can't believe she has the nerve to come back here."

"Why not? She has a right to be here, mama. She was born and raised in Benvenuto, and her family is here."

"And what about *my* family?"

"What about it? Do we have to go through this again? We don't know what happened to him, mama. We probably never will. He may have abandoned us or he may be dead, but papa did not run off to America with Eva Amadeo."

Natalia shot a venomous look at her daughter. "Finish counting," she said as she stormed towards the shop door.

Out in the morning sunshine, Natalia leaned against the shop wall and watched the people of Benvenuto go about their business. She envied them their mundane tasks, free from the kind of inner storm she was battling. Hers was a tempest that had begun long ago, and which, although tapered by the passing of the years, had never fully died. She knew that Luciano would never have left her and his children if he had not been coerced by the charms of a younger woman. There could be no other explanation. People didn't just disappear. The Amadeos had always denied this, of course, but now Eva was back, and Natalia was determined to get a confession from her.

Chapter 6

May 10

In all her years in America, Eva's memory of the night sky above the mountains had always remained as clear as the sky itself. Leaning on the windowsill in her childhood bedroom, the window open to the fresh night air, she tried counting the stars like she had as a child until she inevitably lost her place, a happy nostalgia swirling up from her past to put a smile on her lips. Behind her, Stella sat on one of the room's twin beds, humming as she browsed through a guidebook of Italy.

"I really want to visit the Vatican Museums when we get to Rome," said Stella. "What do you think?"

"I think you should see whatever you want to see." Like Stella, Eva was looking forward to spending a day in Rome. They would fly home from there at the end of their trip.

"We can split up and go sightseeing separately if you don't want to go with me."

"There's plenty of time to plan it out," said Eva. "Let's just enjoy being here for now."

From the foyer downstairs came the sound of guests arriving, friends and relatives Eva's mother had invited for coffee and cake in honor of Eva and Stella's arrival.

The aroma of freshly perked espresso drifted up from the kitchen as Maria's voice rose from the foot of the stairs calling them to come down.

In the living room, the credenza was set with china dessert plates, bottles of assorted liquors, and a selection of cakes and cookies. When Eva and Stella entered the room, they were crushed into a round of hugs and kisses. No one knew Stella but that didn't matter. When Umberto introduced her as Maria's sister's daughter, she received the same affectionate attention as Eva. The older people had known Maria's sister, Efemia, long before she moved to America as a young bride with Alberto to make a new life in New York.

Each embrace Eva received was its own homecoming, and after everyone had settled down into armchairs, sofas, and folding chairs brought out to accommodate the guests, she took in each face individually, warming with the memories as the room buzzed with chatter. Enzo the barber was there with his wife Louisa and a toddler they introduced as their granddaughter, a person not yet born when Eva had lived in Benvenuto. Giacomo and his sister Giacometta were two cousins on their father's side— Giacomo a bachelor, Giacometta married with two sons in the military and a husband who worked abroad. The cousins' mother, Griselda, was home with an illness, but their father Guido had come, a small man with a big laugh who had entertained them with fairytales and funny stories when they were children. Donna Graziella sat in the most comfortable chair in the room. She had been the oldest woman in the town when Eva left, yet there she was now, the lines of her face even deeper and the white hair wispier. Donna Graziella was accompanied by her daughter, Filomena, looking a bit plumper, but with the same kind eyes and pretty face.

Eva knelt beside Donna Graziella, and the old woman caressed Eva's face, repeating over and over how much

Eva had matured into a beautiful young woman. Filomena smiled and nodded in agreement.

"It's so good to see everyone," said Eva.

"You have been missed," said Graziella.

Eva smiled in reply.

"Your mother says you run a café?"

"Yes, the Crystal Café. I'm the manager there."

"And Stella?"

"Stella works in her father's tailor shop in Manhattan. She's an excellent seamstress. One day she's going to take over the business."

"Did I hear my name?" asked Stella as she sidled up beside Eva.

Donna Graziella took Stella's hand. "Is your mother well?" she asked. "I remember how young she was when she left us."

"She's very well. She sends her love to everyone."

Engaged in their conversation, none of them paid attention to the ringing of the doorbell until the conversation in the room waned, drowned out by a commotion coming from the foyer. Eva's heart jumped at the roaring of the visitor trying to barge her way into the house against Maria's protests—the years had not dimmed the sound of Natalia Benini's voice in Eva's memory.

"I demand to see her!" Natalia bellowed as Maria called for her husband.

Umberto sprinted to the door. Eva froze. Stella looked confused, but the rest of the family and friends, silent and embarrassed, looked at one another with frowns and shaking heads.

"Go home," Umberto boomed. "Stop making a fool of yourself."

Natalia's continued shrieking sent Giacomo and Sandro into the hallway.

"Get out," Maria shouted to Natalia, "before I call the

police."

"You call them," Natalia shouted back. "I'm not leaving until I see that disgrace you call a daughter. I have a right to—"

The slamming of the door cut off Natalia's rant, which continued on the doorstep while Maria hurried to the phone in the living room, apologizing to all and no one in particular for the terrible turn the evening had taken. Stella turned to Eva with an open mouth and questioning eyes. Eva pushed past her into the hallway, up the stairs, and into her bedroom, locking the door behind her.

* * *

Natalia was too upset to be embarrassed when the police car came up beside her soon after Maria Amadeo had slammed the door in her face. But she got into the car without a fuss and allowed the two officers to bring her home. It was not until she had shut the front door behind her and was banging about the kitchen making a cup of chamomile tea to calm her that she realized what she had done.

Liliana entered the kitchen, and Natalia turned away, not wanting to meet her daughter's eyes. Liliana's silence made her feel even worse. "Are you going to say something?" Natalia asked. "Or are you just going to stand there and judge me?"

Liliana sighed loudly. "I'm not judging you, mama. What happened?"

"What do you think happened?"

"I think the Amadeos wouldn't let you in their house."

Natalia pulled a cup from the cupboard and placed a teabag in it. "They called the police on me."

"Well, what did you expect? You can't go over to someone's house and threaten them."

"There were no threats. I just told them I wanted to see that . . . that . . ."

"You're going to burn yourself on that kettle, mama. Sit down." Natalia sat down and Liliana poured the boiled water into the cup. "You've got to stop giving yourself grief over Eva Amadeo."

It was a sentiment Natalia had heard many times before from many people, especially from her children. As much as she loved them, she could never stand to listen to either Liliana or Fabiano when it came to their father's disappearance. Although it had hit them hard at first, in time they had come to accept it, something Natalia was never fully able to do.

She took her cup and headed towards the hallway. "Good night, Liliana. I'll have my tea upstairs."

Undressing in the quiet of her bedroom, Natalia removed her printed cotton dress and threw it on a chair. When Luciano had first left, she had worn the black clothes of mourning, not because she thought her husband was dead, but because she felt like a widow. She shouted to anyone who would listen that Luciano was alive and living with Eva Amadeo in America, and that she would wear the widow's clothes until Luciano came to his senses and returned to her. After a few days, however, she abandoned the black because people in town had begun to whisper that she was going a little crazy. She was not going crazy. She had seen them together, Eva and her husband, all those years ago at the outdoor market in Santa Chiara a few weeks before the Feast of San Vito. Natalia was looking over a set of kitchen curtains at one of the stalls when she looked up and saw her husband standing on the sand and Eva walking up to him. She could not hear what they were saying but she could see that they had exchanged words. Yet it was the dreamy look on her husband's face that told Natalia all she needed to know. Later, when she asked Luciano about it, he acted as if he didn't know what she was talking about. She knew then that she would have to keep a sharp eye on both of them.

Natalia slipped on a nightgown and got into bed. Across the room the glass balcony doors overlooking the back yard were open to the night air and the view of the sea far away in the distance. She often lay awake at night staring out at the play of dark blue water against the endless black sky, watching, as if her husband would return at any moment from across the ocean. Now, knowing that Eva Amadeo was in Benvenuto and that Luciano was in America waiting for her, Natalia wondered why she should ever leave that bed again.

* * *

Once Natalia Benini had been escorted home by the local police and the family and friends had gone home to their own houses, nothing disturbed the dark stillness on the street outside the Amadeo house. From her bedroom, Eva heard them leaving in a sad exodus, commiserating with Maria and Umberto as they went. She imagined her parents sitting solemnly in the living room with Sandro and Stella amid the half-empty cups of coffee and soiled napkins that were all that was left of their ruined party. They had tried to coax her out of her room with comforting words and offers of support, but all their pleas had not moved Eva to open the door. She had been humiliated, and worse, had had the full force of a memory she had tried to bury slam into her like a wall of seawater in the form of Natalia Benini and her wild obsession.

When Eva finally went downstairs, she found her mother in the kitchen washing the dessert plates and her father and brother seated at the table in front of cups of coffee, their faces grim. "Where's Stella?" she asked.

Maria dried her hands on a dishtowel and came over to her. "Sit down, Eva. What can I get you? Are you all right?"

"I'm fine. Where's Stella?"

"In the living room," said Sandro. "I don't think she wants to talk to us."

At that moment, Stella walked in, frowning. "No one will tell me what's going on," she said.

Eva sat at the table beside her brother, motioning Stella to join them.

"Stella," said Maria, "can I get you a cup of coffee?"

"No, aunt, I want to know what happened tonight. Who was that woman who came here and why was she acting like that?"

Maria looked at her daughter as if to ask permission to explain. Eva rubbed her palms over her cheeks and sighed. "It's okay, mama. Stella, the woman who came here this evening was Natalia Benini." Umberto put a hand on Eva's wrist. "Really, papa, it's okay." Eva turned to Stella. "Fifteen years ago, her husband Luciano disappeared."

"And she hasn't been right in the head ever since," said Maria.

"Mama, please. It was a terrible thing that happened to her."

"Terrible, yes, but she has no right blaming you."

"Why would she blame you?" asked Stella. "What does she think you did?"

"She thinks I ran off to America with him."

Stella barked an incredulous laugh. "You're kidding me, right? This is a joke?"

No one smiled.

"No joke," said Eva.

"Why would she think that?"

"Because he disappeared just before I left Benvenuto. She put the two things together and came up with a story that she told herself."

"What do you mean by 'disappeared'?"

"Just that," said Sandro. "He left home and never came back."

"Be quiet, Sandro," said Umberto. "We don't need to talk about this." He looked at his wife, who looked at Eva, who chewed her lip.

"Oh, come on," said Stella. "You can't stop now. I want to know what happened."

Eva's stomach clenched again, stirred by memories of those anxious days following the feast when she had waited for the police to come and arrest her.

"There's nothing else to say," said Sandro, looking down at his coffee cup.

"So they never found out what happened to him?" asked Stella.

"No," said Maria. "They never did." She began to twist the end of the dishtowel she was holding.

"That poor woman," said Stella. "It sounds like he deserted her. Although he could have been the victim of a crime, I suppose."

"That's enough talk," said Umberto. "This all happened a long time ago, and we don't pay any attention to Natalia anymore."

Eva stood up from the table. "I'm very tired," she said. "I'm going to bed. Are you coming, Stella?" With an abrupt 'good night' to everyone, she left the kitchen without waiting for Stella to answer.

A short while later, when Stella quietly opened the door to the bedroom, Eva was in bed with the lights out. She pretended to be asleep as Stella undressed. Once Stella was in her own bed, Eva opened her eyes to stare at the moonlit ceiling. She didn't move, waiting for the sound of steady, rhythmic breathing to tell her that Stella had fallen asleep. Instead, Stella's voice came softly out of the semidarkness.

"There's something you're not telling me, isn't there?"

Eva was silent.

"I know you're awake, Eva."

Eva turned on her side to face her cousin.

"When we were talking about that man's disappearance," Stella continued, "your parents and Sandro looked very uncomfortable."

"So what do you think I'm not telling you?"

"All I'm saying is that there's more to this story than just that woman disturbing everybody with her delusions."

"Wouldn't you be disturbed by her? After I left Benvenuto, Natalia ran all over town shouting to anyone who would listen that I ran off with her husband. She persecuted my family for months."

"I get it, but I still think you're hiding something."

Eva remained silent, knowing that Stella deserved better from her. From the first day Eva had arrived in New York all those years ago, Stella had welcomed her warmly and unconditionally. Stella had patiently taught her English, had overlooked Eva's moodiness as the normal behavior of someone living in a new and foreign place. Stella introduced her to the fast foods not found in their mothers' kitchens, to amusement parks and shopping malls, to the sights, sounds, and smells found in the world of an American teenager. And later, as adults, it was Stella who found an apartment in Forest Hills, one of the nicest neighborhoods in Queens, and suggested they share it as roommates. Stella was Eva's best friend.

"Go to sleep, Stella. There is nothing to tell."

Stella turned angrily in bed, her back to her cousin. "Fine," she said, "keep your secrets."

Chapter 7

May 23

Fabiano Benini sat in the oak-paneled window seat in the living room of his Florence apartment watching the sun spreading layers of flaming pink over the still waters of the Arno. On the Ponte Vecchio branching elegantly over the river, shopkeepers began opening their stalls, and the motor sounds of traffic mingling with human voices hummed upwards from the street, muffled by the glass and the distance of four stories. He liked to begin each day this way, sipping American coffee, watching the city awaken, slowly at first, to bloom into a magical riot of activity.

Fabiano was thinking about the intersection of science and art in da Vinci's work, the topic of the lecture he would give to his students at the university the following afternoon, when his phone ringing beside him, a harsh intrusion into the silence of his thoughts, rudely interrupted his morning ritual.

When he answered, his sister's words were preceded by a long and exasperated sigh. "It's mama," she said. "She claims that her ulcer is killing her, even though the doctor says she doesn't have one."

Fabiano frowned. "I bet she blames it on Eva Amadeo."

"Of course she does. Since Eva came back here, she hasn't stopped complaining about her stomach. For the past two weeks she's spent every day in bed and hardly eats anything, even after I cook special foods for her. Eva left yesterday, so I figured that would be the end of it, but no. I had to practically drag her to the doctor to get checked, and he found absolutely nothing wrong with her."

Fabiano recalled the phone call Liliana had made when Eva first arrived in Benvenuto. He had heard the frustration in his sister's voice as she described how their mother had shown up on the Amadeo's doorstep and made a fool of herself in front of a house full of people, how she had to be driven home by the police, and what a disgrace it had been.

Now his sister's voice, hard and longsuffering, jangled across the airwaves again. "She demands to see you, Fabi, and she wouldn't give me any peace until I called you. There's something she wants you to do, but she refuses to tell me what it is."

"Why didn't she call me herself?"

"Who knows? She's been ordering me around like I'm a servant."

"Now Liliana, don't be so hard on her."

"You have to come home, Fabi. I can't take much more of this."

"Is she feeling that bad? Maybe she should go to the hospital."

"Have you been listening to me? I told you she's already seen the doctor. I went with her to have tests done. No ulcer. She's fine. But was she satisfied with that? No. As soon as we left, she kept insisting that she didn't care what the tests said, that she knew her own body better than the doctor did."

"Oh, boy."

"It gets worse. She said she dreamed that Saint Rocco came to her bedside and took her hand—a sign from God that she's seriously ill."

"Is he the patron saint of ulcers?"

"Of pestilence. Pestilence! Like we're living in the Middle Ages."

"Well . . . who can argue with a sign from God?"

"Don't be flippant. It's not a sign from God, it's the ravings of an angry and stubborn woman. Next thing you know she's going to ask me to call Father Pietro to come over and administer the last rites. Please, Fabi, you have to come home. She insists, and as much as I love her, I have lost my patience with her nonsense."

Fabiano ran his fingers through his hair and sighed. In the absence of their father, he had taken on the responsibilities of the man of the house, even though at the time of his father's disappearance he had already left to study in the north. He had cared for his mother and sister from afar to the best of his ability, yet he had never completely shaken off the twinge of guilt he harbored at remaining so far away from Benvenuto.

"Let me talk to her," he said. "Maybe we can settle this over the phone."

"She wants to see you, Fabi. She won't budge on this."

"Just ask her to get on the phone."

Fabiano ignored his sister's muttered swears as he waited for her to walk to their mother's room. After a few moments, raised voices told him that Liliana was having no luck convincing Natalia to speak to him.

"Did you hear all that?" asked Liliana when she got back. "She insists that she needs to speak to you in person. There is some big important thing going on—only she and God knows what—that she can't tell me about."

"Did you ask her why?"

"What do you think? Of course I did. All she said was that I would try to talk her out of it, and that she didn't want to waste her time arguing with me because she's aggravated enough as it is."

"This is ridiculous."

"You need to come home."

"Okay," he said with a loud exhale. "It's not exactly a short drive, you know. I'll leave this morning, but first I'll have to make arrangements with the university to have someone take over my classes. And I won't be able to stay long, Liliana. I have responsibilities here."

"Just come, Fabi. Please." The next thing he heard was silence as Liliana ended the call.

Fabiano leaned back on the window seat and sipped his coffee. It had been many months since he had been back in Benvenuto. Home, his true place of belonging, was not in the rugged landscape of the south, but in Florence, where his position as professor of Renaissance art kept him busy and fulfilled. He owed his success to the priest, Father Pietro, who had seen his potential early on, had encouraged him to study hard, and, perhaps more importantly, had encouraged his mother to let him go. He had been fortunate, and now he had to repay some of that fortune with a little sacrifice.

* * *

The day had begun with bickering. It was their first and only full day in Rome, and Stella accused Eva of taking too long getting ready, that she was wasting the little time they were to have in the Eternal City. They had spent a full two weeks in Benvenuto without further grievance from Natalia Benini. In fact, they had not seen or heard from her since that night when she came to the house. They had celebrated with Sandro and Gianna at their wedding, had spent time with friends and family, had visited some of the local sights for Stella's sake, and left Benvenuto late the morning before, arriving in Rome after a nearly six-hour drive. Their lodging was a simple but charming *pensione* a few blocks from St. Peter's Basilica. After a dinner of pizza and wine at a local trattoria followed by a leisurely walk along the Via della Conciliazione, past the Castel Sant'Angelo, and over the St. Angelo Bridge, they had returned to the *pensione*. They wanted to get a good night's rest so they could throw themselves into the Roman experience early and refreshed the next morning.

But Eva's idea of the Roman experience was different from Stella's. Stella insisted she would not leave Rome without seeing the Vatican Museums, while Eva wanted only to walk around the city, enjoy the spring air, and sit in an outdoor café with some coffee and perhaps a pastry as she watched the citizens of Rome go about their business. Eva, though, had agreed to go to the museums to appease her cousin and was regretting it now, as she found herself in a stifling crowd shuffling from one gallery to the next and hardly able to see anything for the sea of bodies pressing in on all sides.

"I can barely breathe, Stella. And if one more person pushes against me . . ."

"Stop complaining. You're in one of the most magnificent places in the world. You're surrounded by masterworks created by some of the most gifted artists in history, and all you can do is moan. If you have to suffer a little crowding to experience this . . ." Stella's words trailed off as they passed through the entryway to the Sistine Chapel. Suddenly they were surrounded by color overtaking every inch of the walls and ceiling. Dynamic, fluid scenes graced every cornice and crevice, and at the center of it all was Michelangelo's famous, enormous fresco of flesh tones and vibrant blues dominating the wall above the altar.

"Look up," said Stella after she had found her voice again. Eva looked up to see God creating the universe in a series of tableaus, but her eye was quickly drawn back to the central fresco at the front of the chapel, to the powerful figure of Christ, his mother beside him, overseeing the final fate of humankind. Figures rising from their graves rose to heaven assisted by angels, while the damned were pushed and pulled downward into the waiting boat of Charon to be ferried without hope into hell. These were the souls who had never repented, their sins unforgiven because they had never suffered remorse.

Eva's head hurt. She blamed the overwhelming crowd. Too many people suffocating her. Not enough air for all of them to breathe properly in this enclosed space. "I'll meet you outside," she said.

"But you've only been here a few minutes."

"Outside, Stella. Outside of the museum. I'll meet you there. You stay as long as you like."

Eva took one last look at The Last Judgment and left the chapel. After finding her way to the exit and stepping into the sunshine of St. Peter's Square, she leaned against one of the colossal pillars. The Square was busy with tourists, local Romans, and a host of priests and nuns. Life was everywhere, each person with his and her own secrets and regrets. Where would each have been placed in the fresco, she wondered, ascending to the waiting angels or falling to the fire below? Eva wondered where she herself would have been placed. She sat down at the base of the pillar and waited.

After what seemed an impossibly long time, Stella came walking across the Square.

"Are you feeling okay?" she asked when she reached Eva. "You looked a little pale in there."

"I'm fine. I just needed some air. Let's get lunch."

They chose to eat outdoors at a small trattoria tucked away on a side street. The little table was set with flower-patterned china and a small vase of primroses.

"You know," said Stella after the waiter had taken their order, "I'm so inspired. I think I'm going to design some new dress patterns based on some of the paintings I've seen. The combination of colors in those masterpieces is amazing."

"Speaking of that, you promised last month to make a new spring blazer for me."

"I haven't forgotten. It's just been so busy in the tailor shop. I'll start on it this week, after we get back home. I promise."

When the waiter arrived with their salads, Eva looked away from Stella to see a man wearing jeans and a blue work shirt leaving the restaurant. He had barely stepped outside when he turned around and reentered as if he had forgotten something.

Eva stiffened.

"What's wrong?" asked Stella.

Moments later, when the man reappeared and passed their table, Eva shot up, knocking the table's edge, rattling the china and sending the little vase of primroses crashing to the pavement. The man looked shocked and was about to say something when Eva ran into the trattoria and shut herself in the restroom.

"Eva! What's going on?" Stella's worried voice came through the door. "Are you all right?"

When Eva opened the door, everyone in the restaurant was turned towards the two of them, staring. The waiter who had taken their order came over and asked anxiously if the *signora* was all right.

"That man," said Eva, "the one with the blue shirt who passed our table outside, is he still there?"

"No, *signora*, he's gone. Did he say something to you?"

"Do you know him?"

"Yes, he comes here sometimes for lunch."

"Do you know his name?"

The waiter looked confused and hesitant to answer. "Yes," he said slowly, eyeing Eva suspiciously. "His name is Bruno. He's the gardener at the Casa di Santa Rosalia."

"Gardener?"

"The gardener at the convent guest house. What's wrong, *signora*?"

"What's going on?" demanded Stella.

"I need to get out of here." Eva pushed past Stella, the waiter, and the watching diners and rushed out the door, not stopping until she reached the *pensione* and the security of her room.

* * *

The Casa di Santa Rosalia's garden was one of the most faithfully pruned gardens in Rome. Luciano made sure of it. It had become his when the Casa's former gardener retired many years earlier and Luciano was offered, and gratefully accepted, the position. Luciano made sure that the fountain at its center, a simple marble bowl on a pedestal of sculpted marble roses, was kept free of any debris or dirt by his daily polishing with a soft cloth. The large square of grass on which the fountain sat was always neatly mowed and watered, and the border of lemon trees and the colorful flower beds with their rows of peonies, primroses, violets, and buttercups, was always lovingly pruned and fed with quality fertilizer. Even the iron benches, with their intricate scrollwork, placed at intervals along the border looked elegant and pristine because of the tireless efforts of his polishing cloth. This square of Eden, this perfectly manicured bit of Paradise was his haven. Here he felt peace, and with that peace came an indifference to the love of wine that had caused so many problems in his past.

But the garden offered no peace today. Today, Luciano was deeply disturbed by the sight of Eva Amadeo, whom he had half frightened to death in the trattoria. He might not have even seen her if he hadn't gone back into the restaurant to retrieve his phone, which he had left at his table. He had simply gone into the restaurant to have lunch because, as much as he liked the food at the Casa, he sometimes preferred to enjoy meals prepared by other chefs. He did not expect to come face to face with Eva.

What was she doing in Rome? Had she come looking for him after all this time? And how could she know where to find him? All these years past, he still could not clearly remember the details of what had happened on the night of the Feast of San Vito. His drunkenness at the time had impaired him, had robbed him of ever fully knowing what he might have done to Eva. He knew that he had been wandering the countryside as the festival carried on in town, that he had come across Eva sitting alone on a rock on the outskirts of Benvenuto, and that she had been crying. He remembered she wore yellow, but whether a dress or a blouse he could not recall, and a white lace shawl was wrapped around her shoulders. And he remembered reaching out to her before plunging into the ravine. When he awakened from unconsciousness in the moonlight, bloodied and bruised from the fall, Eva was gone, and on the ground was her blood-stained shawl.

Luciano paced the length of the garden, trying to recall the features of the woman's face in the trattoria. It had all happened so quickly. All he had done was pass her table and she bolted. Perhaps it wasn't Eva after all, just a woman who looked like her. Perhaps he reminded her of someone she knew, someone she feared or abhorred. Luciano puzzled over the possibility. It was nothing to be concerned about, he concluded. If it had been more than nothing, then something would have happened.

* * *

Eva did not stay long at the *pensione*. She knew Stella would follow her, would find her there and demand answers, and Eva needed space to think, not answer questions. Grabbing her purse, she left the room, hoping a brisk walk would calm her nerves and clear her head, because what she had seen in the restaurant was something she could not make sense of.

What she had seen was the ghost of Luciano Benini. Only it was not a ghost. It was a flesh-and-blood man, older now and a few pounds heavier, his black hair grayer, but the face was his, the strong jaw and bright blue eyes under dark heavy lashes. Yet it could not be Luciano because Luciano was dead.

Eva wandered aimlessly past shops and houses, along the Tiber, and into the narrow streets of Trastevere until she came to a piazza and sat on the steps of a church. Taking her phone from her purse, she tapped her father's number and waited for him to answer.

"Is everything all right?" asked Umberto. "Did you get to Rome okay?"

"We got to Rome just fine, papa."

"Then what is it? Are you and Stella all right?"

"Stella and I are fine." Eva stopped to take a breath. "Papa, I think I saw Luciano Benini today."

There was silence on the other end before Umberto's voice came calm and measured. "What do you mean?"

"I saw him, papa, in a restaurant here in Rome. I asked the waiter if he knew him. He said he was a gardener at one of the convent guest houses."

"It can't be him."

"They never found his body, papa. *You* didn't find it when you went to look for him that night. We still don't know what happened to him."

"Where is Stella?"

"I don't know. Looking for me, probably. I'm on the street now. I don't know what to do."

"There's nothing to do. You were mistaken, Eva. It was just someone who resembled him."

Eva's tight nerves loosened. "Do you really think so, papa?"

"Go back to your hotel and relax. Have a nice night out with Stella and forget all this. Luciano is gone, and none of it was your fault."

Chapter 8

It was evening by the time Eva returned to the *pensione*, where she found Stella in a fit of fury. When Eva had rushed out of the restaurant, Stella had hurriedly paid the bill and tried to follow, but Eva was gone by the time Stella got to the street. When she got back to the *pensione*, Eva was not there. Stella had walked all over Rome trying to find her, much to her concern and frustration, and this was the tirade Eva now listened to as she sat on the bed in their room with Stella hovering over her, arms flailing.

"How many times do I have to tell you I'm sorry?" asked Eva.

"I don't care if you're sorry! I want an explanation!"

"And you deserve one. But it's complicated."

"Do you think I'm too stupid to understand complicated?"

Eva motioned Stella towards a chair beside the dresser. "Sit down."

"I'm too angry to sit down."

"Okay, then . . . Remember in Benvenuto when you said there was something I wasn't telling you?"

"Of course I remember."

"Well, you were right." Eva took a deep breath and

looked up at her cousin. "Really, Stella, you need to sit down for this."

Stella walked to the dresser, leaned against it, and waited for Eva to continue.

"That conversation we had in my mother's kitchen," said Eva, "about Luciano Benini and how he disappeared all those years ago . . ."

"And his wife thinking you were responsible for it?"

Eva nodded. "Well, I was, but not in the way she thinks."

Stella frowned. "What are you talking about?"

"I was with him on the night he disappeared."

Stella's eyes widened.

"And I never told you because I wanted to forget all about it."

"Forget about what? What happened?"

After searching for the right words, Eva began her story. She was able to recall every detail of that evening, relive every emotion, from her despair at seeing the doctor's son with another girl, to her horror and fear at the sight of Luciano lying lifeless at the bottom of the ravine. When she had finished, Stella stared silently at her for a long while.

"For God's sake, Stella, say something."

"So you think you killed him?"

"He was never found, so I thought he must have crawled away and died somewhere."

"That doesn't seem possible. How can a body just remain lying on the ground with no one discovering it?"

"I don't know. Maybe he was eaten by animals."

Stella walked to the window. Outside, the sky was beginning to darken into evening. "So that's the real reason you came to America?"

"Yes. My father thought Luciano would show up eventually and when he didn't, well, I started to get sick. My nerves were shot. I couldn't eat. My parents insisted

I go away for a while."

With a deep sigh, Stella came over to Eva and sat down beside her on the bed. "And you've been keeping this terrible memory to yourself all this time," she said. "My poor cousin."

Eva leaned her head on Stella's shoulder. "I'm so sorry, Stella. I just wanted to bury it."

"I get it. I also don't think you killed anybody."

Eva lifted her head to look at her cousin.

"There's something wrong with this story, Eva. I just can't put my finger on it. And what does this have to do with you running out of the restaurant today?"

"Because I thought I saw him. That man who passed our table, I thought it was Luciano."

"The man the waiter said was the gardener at the, what did he call it . . . Santa Rosa?

"Santa Rosalia."

"The man you supposedly killed?"

"Yes. I'm almost sure it was him."

"Almost?"

"Yes."

"Then I guess we have to go and see for ourselves."

* * *

Luciano sat on his favorite bench at the end of the garden and looked around approvingly at the fruits of his work in the fading light. Soon the light bulbs strung among the trees and along the borders would turn on automatically and bathe the garden in a soft yellow glow. Now that he had reflected on the events of that afternoon, he decided he would give no more thought to Eva Amadeo. Even if it had been Eva in that trattoria, it didn't matter anymore. His dealings with her had ended fifteen years ago on the night of the Feast of San Vito.

Luciano would go to bed early. A good night's rest would make him feel better, and the morning sunshine when he awakened would dispel any shadows cast by his past. But first he would have a glass of the iced lemonade made fresh daily by the sisters, which he often enjoyed on warm nights. He knew that all he had to do was enter the kitchen and if there was a sister present, she would pour him a glass without even asking. He loved their lemonade, and they knew it. He was a lucky man to be so well treated.

As Luciano entered the foyer through the French doors that led to the garden, he noticed two women walk up to the sister at the reception desk, and to his surprise they were the same women from the trattoria. The black-haired one, the one he thought might have been Eva, looked nervous and was wringing her hands. Luciano backed away and positioned himself between the door jamb and the outside wall, trying to remain hidden as he peeked in and listened to the conversation at the desk. The second of the two visitors, the one with a brown ponytail, asked for him by name, but not his real name. She asked for Bruno.

"I can see if he's in his room," said the sister, sounding perplexed, and Luciano knew why. He had no friends here, no relations. No one ever came to the Casa looking for him. "Are you friends of his?"

The one with the ponytail responded. "No," she said, "we just wanted to ask him something."

The sister looked suspicious. "May I ask what this is about?"

"It's personal."

The sister gave her a hard look as she reached for the phone.

Luciano's stomach churned when the phone in his pocket rang.

"He's not answering," said the sister as she hung up. "If you leave your name and a number where he can reach you, I'll give him a message."

The black-haired one seemed to relax, but the one with the ponytail was not so easily swayed. "May we look around the grounds?" she asked. "Maybe he's somewhere around."

"If you're not a guest here, we can't allow you to walk around," said the sister.

"Why not?"

The sister looked annoyed. "Because you're not a guest here."

"Fine. We'd like a room, then." She pulled out a credit card as the black-haired one began to protest.

"I'm sorry," said the sister. "There are no rooms available this evening."

Luciano felt like a coward hiding in the shadows by the door. He walked into the foyer. "Please," he said to the sister as he approached, "let them through."

Both women turned. The black-haired one looked stunned, almost petrified, and Luciano's chest sizzled with nerves when he saw her face. She was, indeed, Eva Amadeo.

"Ladies," he said, his stomach doing somersaults, "please come this way."

He led them into the garden. When they reached a bench, he turned around and motioned for them to sit. They remained standing. Neither woman said anything, just stood before him, serious and expectant.

"You seem to know who I am," he said, trying hard to keep his composure, "but I don't know either of you."

He didn't want to lie, but it was a matter of self-preservation. Luciano had been taken by surprise for a second time that day, and he was unprepared to face Eva Amadeo and the consequences of what he might have done fifteen years ago on a rock above a deep ravine in the mountains of the south.

The one with the ponytail kept looking at Eva, then at him, then back again to Eva, who had a face of stone, staring like a child intrigued by a stranger. Finally, the one with the ponytail spoke. "We're sorry to bother you. We saw you in the restaurant today and asked the waiter if he knew where we could find you because my cousin here may have acted rudely. She wants to apologize."

Luciano was unconvinced. "You were willing to book a room for the night just to make sure I got an apology?"

"Oh," she said, "so you heard that?"

"Why is it so urgent that you speak to me? And why did your cousin look so frightened when she saw me this afternoon? Tell me what's going on here."

Luciano looked from one to the other, bolder now that he was sure Eva didn't recognize him. In fact, she seemed incapable of speech.

"My name is Eva Amadeo," she said suddenly, as if gathering all her strength to make this declaration. "I come from a town called Benvenuto. Do you know it?" As she spoke, she continued to stare into his face as if it were the most interesting thing in the world.

Luciano's chest burned. "Should I know it?"

"Maybe."

"I don't know this place. Look, if you have something to say, then say it. Do I know you? I don't recall ever seeing either of you, so if you know something I don't, then tell me."

The one with the ponytail interjected. "Well, Eva?"

"I have nothing to say except that I'm sorry if I was rude to you today."

Luciano accepted the apology with a nod and a forced smile. After the women left the garden, he stood staring after them for several seconds before lowering himself onto the bench beside him, overwhelmed with relief and shame.

* * *

"So now you know," said Stella as she and Eva walked back into the foyer of the Casa di Santa Rosalia. "It wasn't him after all. Which doesn't help you, though. The mystery still remains as to what happened to Luciano, but honestly, Eva, you don't really think you're responsible for the man's death, do you?"

Eva didn't say a word as they passed through the foyer and out into the street. Standing before the door to the Casa, she turned to her cousin and shook her head. "It's him," she said.

"What!"

"It's Luciano. It has to be. The eyes, I remember those eyes. Such a deep blue."

"Then why did you say—"

"I don't know. I couldn't believe it. I couldn't say anything. He was so insistent."

"Are you absolutely sure?"

"Yes."

"Then you have to go back in there and talk to him."

"No!" Eva sank to the street and leaned against the wall of the Casa. "I don't feel well," she said, clutching her stomach. "Cramps."

Stella bent down and put her arm around her cousin's shoulder. "Let's go back inside," she said. "You can't sit out here in the street."

"No, please. I just need a moment." Eva breathed rapidly, head down, as thoughts crashed through her brain. All these years she had lived with the guilt of having sent a man to his death, and in one day all she had believed about her greatest sin was shattered. Relief vied with confusion, happiness clashed with remorse for a

72

youth tainted by mental and emotional suffering. What could have happened to bring Luciano Benini here to Rome, to take on a new identity as a gardener in a guest house? And what part had she played in it? He claimed not to know her, yet she knew she hadn't changed that much. And why had he denied knowing the name of the town he had lived in most of his life?

Gradually, Eva's breathing steadied, and she lifted herself up with Stella's help.

"Can you walk?" asked Stella.

Eva nodded.

Stella took Eva by the arm and led her down the street. As they rounded the corner to walk the back streets leading to the *pensione*, Eva got the feeling they were being followed. "He's behind us," she said, stopping abruptly and looking over her shoulder. "He's following us."

Stella looked back, still holding Eva's arm. "There's no one there," she said.

"I can feel it," said Eva. "He's there."

Stella forcefully pulled Eva forward. "I'm starting to really worry about you, Eva."

On the next street they came across a group of young men standing around laughing and talking outside a noisy café.

"Maybe they can check," said Eva. "I'll ask them to see if someone is following us."

"Eva, stop it!" Stella pulled Eva past the men and through the warren of streets without another word. As they neared the *pensione*, Stella ordered Eva to go to their room and stay there while she went out and got them something to eat. Neither had had any food since Eva ran out of the trattoria that afternoon.

"I'll come with you," said Eva.

"You said you had cramps. And besides, you're in no mental state to go anywhere right now."

"I'm feeling better. The walk helped." Stella looked skeptical but Eva insisted. "And I want to eat at the trattoria we ate at this afternoon."

"Are you kidding me? Back to the scene of the crime? No way."

Eva was not to be swayed. She knew she was acting erratically, one minute confident and confrontational, the next anxious and paranoid, but she could not tame the conflicting thoughts that swerved through her brain. Reality was playing tricks on her, and it seemed impossible to separate what was true from what she was imagining. In one day she had seen a presumably dead man alive, only to find that he denied his own existence. He had tried to convince her that he was not the man she thought he was, even as she saw with her own eyes that he was. Perhaps at the restaurant she could learn more.

Eva pulled Stella in the direction of the trattoria and Stella, with an exasperated sigh, followed. When they got there, they took the same table they had occupied earlier that afternoon, only now the sunshine that had lit up the street was replaced by the glow of amber lights spilling out from the restaurant and from the windows of nearby homes and shops. The staff had changed shifts since their earlier meal, and Eva didn't see the waiter who had told her about the gardener at the Casa di Santa Rosalia.

"Are you sure you're okay with this?" asked Stella as she opened her menu. "No more fits of panic with you running away and worrying me to death?"

"I'm fine. Let's just order."

"I don't know why you wanted to come back here. You're not going to find out anything new, you know. It's not like Luciano works here. He's just a customer."

"Why do you have to be so pessimistic? I'm doing everything I can to make sense of what's been happening. Aren't you the least bit curious to find out what's going on?"

"I know what's going on. You said it's Luciano, so it's Luciano. He was obviously lying to us."

"Yes, but why?"

"Who cares? For fifteen years you've been carrying around all this guilt and now you can drop it, so why can't you just leave it at that and be happy?"

"Because what if I'm wrong?"

"Oh, jeez!" Stella threw up her hands. "Now you're not sure?"

Eva looked away, embarrassed and frustrated. Memory was not foolproof. Maybe hers was faulty and this gardener was a dead ringer for Luciano. She could not go back to New York without at least trying to find out more about this Bruno at the Casa di Santa Rosalia.

The waiter approached and took their order. Before he left the table Eva asked if he ever worked the day shift.

"Yes, *signora*. Why do you ask?"

"There's a man who comes in here sometimes, a gardener at one of the convent guest houses. I was wondering if you knew him."

The waiter smiled and nodded. "Yes, yes. Bruno. A very nice man. Quiet. He keeps to himself, but we all know him here. Is he a friend of yours?"

"Yes, an old friend. I was wondering if he ever talks about the town he comes from, or about his family."

"I don't think so, *signora*. As far as I know he's always lived in Rome, and he never mentions family."

Eva thanked him as he left the table, then turned to Stella, who had said nothing to the waiter other than that she wanted a salad and a plate of pasta Bolognese. "I guess that's it then," said Eva. "I guess this is where the story ends."

"Unless you want to go back to the guest house."

"It would make no difference. Bruno or Luciano, we would get the same response."

They ate mostly in silence after that, absorbing the

quietly festive atmosphere of the street, knowing this was their last night in Italy. Tomorrow, when they were back in their own home, this whole situation would seem like a dream.

* * *

After the women had left, Luciano, in a fit of remorse, had run after them into the street to tell them he had lied to them, that he really was Luciano Benini from Benvenuto. But cowardice drew him back quickly, and he returned to the guest house and to the refuge of his room before they could discover he had followed them.

Despite his comfortable, peaceful life at the Casa, the possibility of his having committed a terrible crime had always remained hidden in the back of Luciano's mind. The memory of Eva's bloody shawl and the thought that he might have hurt her still haunted him.

Hazy though the memory was, he could recall bits and pieces of the moments directly before his accident—his arm reaching out to Eva, her pushing him away, his loss of balance, and his slipping descent. It played in his mind like a blurry silent film. Had she mistaken his reaching as an unwanted advance and struggled against him, and had he, in trying to balance himself, struck out at her? He could not remember. He could not recall any forceful contact with Eva's body, but the shawl told a different, more sinister story.

If he had harmed her, it would not have been on purpose. Violence was not in his nature. Yet she would not have known that. How could she? She was just a girl at the time, confronted by a grown man who had drunk way too much and who had no right to touch her. At least that's the way Luciano imagined she would have reacted.

Had Eva Amadeo now come to Rome looking to right an injustice? And if so, why had she waited so long?

* * *

It was late evening when Fabiano reached Benvenuto and parked his yellow Fiat in front of his mother's house. When he rang the bell, Liliana opened it and hugged him tightly.

He dropped his duffle bag in the hallway and followed Liliana upstairs. "Who's been taking care of the store?" he asked.

"Uncle Maurizio. He's been such a big help to me, since I now have to wait on mama hand and foot."

The evening's waning sunlight filtered through the glass balcony doors in Natalia's bedroom and fell across the bed, across the sheet-swathed legs of his mother sitting up against an ornately carved oak headboard. Natalia's hair, thick and streaked with gray, brushed the level plane of her shoulders, framing an oval face. Even as she aged, Natalia's beauty remained.

As soon as Fabiano entered the room, Natalia's arms reached out to him. He bent over her, and she kissed him on his cheeks and forehead before releasing him onto a chair beside the bed.

Liliana stood leaning against the doorjamb. "I have to bring her meals to her, and most of the time she won't eat."

Natalia turned to Fabiano. "My stomach is rotting. The sight of that woman, after all these years . . . She put me in this bed."

"Eva Amadeo did not put you in that bed," said Liliana loudly. "I've had enough. You deal with her Fabi." Liliana waved her hand in dismissal and left the room.

Alone with his mother, Fabiano did not know what to say. He watched her stare ahead out the balcony doors to the lowering sun, to the sliver of shimmering sea visible far across and below the mountain. When she said nothing, he offered a modest consolation. "Liliana is doing her best, mama."

Natalia ignored him, her face as stiff and cold as any of the marble masterpieces Fabiano projected onto the screen of his darkened classroom.

"The doctor says you're not as sick as you think you are, so you can't blame her for being upset. She's worried about you."

Natalia's eyes narrowed and her lips became a straight line. He placed a hand on her arm but received no response. After a long silence, she smiled—a thin, insipid twitch of the mouth.

"What can any doctor know about a woman's suffering?"

Fabiano nodded, painfully aware of his mother's chronic heartache since his father's disappearance. It was a slow, cold ache that moved with her through the years and seemed to never warm into anything better than a subtle bitterness. Yet she seemed to have accepted it in time, an unhappy consequence of fate. And now here it was again, claiming her peace of mind and making her physically sick. "What can I do for you?" he asked.

"I need your help."

"Of course, mama. Anything."

"I want you to go to America and find your father."

Fabiano was not sure he had heard her correctly. It seemed that the air around him had suddenly gelled, freezing the moment and his mother's words.

"What? How?"

"Find her and you'll find him."

"She was just here."

"Did you think she would bring him, Fabi?"

His mother's expression looked so pained, so pathetic, that Fabiano began to fear the weakness of his own will.

"You want me to go to America? All the way to America?"

"Yes."

"But I have classes . . ."

"Is there no one else in that big university who can teach your classes? Tell them you have a family emergency."

Fabiano heard Liliana preparing coffee in the kitchen downstairs. The smell of it floated up the stairway and into his nostrils like incense. He wanted to bolt from the room, fly down into the kitchen and sit with his sister at the table with a fresh plate of biscotti before him, pretending this conversation with his mother was not happening, that her request was only a joke to chastise him for his infrequent visits home. Instead, he placed his hand on his mother's arm and pleaded.

"What could I possibly find out in America that would make any difference? It wouldn't change anything."

"You could find out the truth. Prove to this town that I'm not the crazy woman they think I am. He was not a cruel man, your father, so go find him and find out why he did this to us."

"And if he's not there? Then what? We don't even know if he's still alive."

"He's there."

"But what if he's not?

"I want answers, and you'll find them when you find Eva Amadeo."

Fabiano sat silently for a long time, staring across the bed to the far wall, deliberately not looking at his mother. "After all this time, mama? You're asking a lot of me."

"You're my son."

"I don't even know where to find her."

"She lives with that cousin of hers in New York. She runs a business there, some kind of coffee bar, or something. Amadeo is always bragging about her."

As Natalia continued to give him instructions on where he might find Eva, Fabiano stopped paying attention. Placing his head in his hands, he combed his fingers through his hair, then rose from his mother's bedside and walked slowly to the balcony doors. Far away and below, the waters of the Ionian glistened the color of blood oranges in the sunset.

Chapter 9

May 24

When Natalia came downstairs for breakfast fully dressed, her hair neatly combed and braided, her children seemed mildly shocked.

"I was just about to bring your breakfast up to you," said Liliana. She was standing at the counter, placing chunks of bread into a bowl of warm milk.

"No, I don't want breakfast. Just coffee."

Liliana frowned as Natalia picked up the espresso pot from the stove and poured the coffee into a small cup. "You shouldn't drink that if your stomach is bothering you," she said.

Natalia nodded and walked out of the kitchen, taking the steaming cup with her.

Fabiano followed her outside to the backyard where several chairs were arranged beneath the sprawling branches of a large pine tree. "You look well," he said. He waved away Natalia's offer to sit in the chair beside her. "I promised to have breakfast with Liliana. I just wanted to make sure you were okay."

"I'm feeling much better today."

"Good."

"I know I made a fool of myself at Amadeo's when Eva turned up, and I regret it, but it won't matter after you bring your father home to us. And when you do, I promise to be a better wife."

"You were a good wife, mama. You wanted what was best for him. For all of us."

"I could have been more patient with him. You know, there were times when he seemed so distant, as if he were in a daydream. I never understood it. Sometimes I would ask him a question and he couldn't answer because he hadn't been listening. I just wanted him to be present more. Do you understand?"

"I think so."

"And he drank too much. That really used to bother me."

"Was it really that bad? I know he sometimes had more than he should have, but it's not like he was an alcoholic."

Natalia shook her head. "It was not good for him, Fabi. I was afraid he would ruin his health. He hadn't always been that way, not in the beginning, not until years later."

"People's habits change. I'm sure it had nothing to do with you." Fabiano bent down and kissed his mother on the cheek. "I'm going back inside now."

As she watched her son walk away, Natalia wondered what her husband was doing at that very moment. Despite his abandonment, she still could not stop caring for him. They had been happy once, in the early days of their life together. They were only teenagers when they had first met, Luciano, a boy from the region's capital visiting relatives in the country, and Natalia, spending the summer with her grandparents in their farmhouse a few miles outside of Benvenuto. One day Natalia went for a walk, followed by one of her grandfather's goats. Luciano later described how he had ventured out on his cousin's best mare that very same day, how at first Natalia was just a speck in the distance until he got closer and the speck became a shapely figure in an orange dress.

Natalia walked casually with the goat beside her, enjoying the last rays of the setting sun.

"Good evening," he said, riding up alongside her.

She looked straight ahead. "I don't know you," she said without changing her pace.

"Not now, maybe, but you will." He smiled confidently and looked away into the distance.

Natalia knew he didn't notice her hands reaching for the goat's neck or see her untie the bronze bell that hung there. So he seemed shocked when the tinkling chunk of metal came hurtling at him, smashing into the left side of his jaw. He did not try to stop her as she ran, pulling the goat beside her, all the way back to her grandparents' house.

They were married three years later in the church at Benvenuto. That autumn, Natalia conceived Fabiano. He grew in her belly like a plump, ripening peach, feeding by way of her body on the finest, freshest foods that Luciano brought into the house. By late spring, Natalia's middle had swollen to bursting, and the heaviness of her body kept her more and more confined to the cool stone walls of their home. She moved lovingly through the rooms each day, cleaning, cooking, shifting things around to make a space for the baby. Nights she spent quietly upstairs listening to the muffled sounds of hammer and saw while Luciano worked at a surprise in the cellar. One night the muffled sounds ceased, and she heard him slowly making his way up the stairs and into the kitchen, struggling, as if he were carrying something bulky and hard to maneuver. When she went into the kitchen, there on the floor beside a dusty, sweaty Luciano sat the gracefully carved curves of a cradle. Crafted of fine mahogany, it was polished to a shine, with a series of delicately carved stars and crescents decorating the edge of its hood.

And now that loving father and husband was gone. Natalia sat quietly in the shade of the pine tree. She sipped the espresso and winced as the liquid hit her stomach. It tasted bitter. She should have listened to Liliana when she told her not to have the coffee. Where did this stubborn streak that ran through her like a taught cord come from? Sometimes it was her worst enemy.

* * *

Fabiano sat on a bench in the piazza with his laptop on his knees searching for reasonably priced flights to New York and finding that there were none. At such short notice, and at this time of year, the costs were well beyond what he wanted to pay. Yet he was willing to overpay for a plane ticket and travel across the ocean if it meant giving his mother some peace, although he harbored no delusion of finding his father. He would make the most of this trip to New York, a city he had often thought of visiting. There were world-class museums there and restaurants serving foods from around the world. There were Broadway theaters and historical landmarks. He would find Eva Amadeo, have a short conversation with her for the sake of his mother, and spend the rest of his time enjoying the city before returning home to tell Natalia that Eva was innocent of adultery. After returning to Italy, he would spend a day or two with Liliana before going back to Florence. He hadn't realized until he arrived in Benvenuto how much he had missed her company.

It was Liliana who had phoned him at the university the day Luciano disappeared. Their father was gone, she said. What did she mean "gone"? Was he dead? She didn't know. She knew only that he had not come home the night before and that their mother was distraught. There had to be a rational explanation, he told her. Luciano was known to go off on his own at times, although he had never spent a night away from home before. Sometimes as a boy, when Fabiano wandered away from town to ramble in the countryside, he would come across his father in some far-off spot, slowly walking or sitting in the grass daydreaming. Luciano would call him over and together they would enjoy the quiet and the sparkle of the sun on the leaves as birds flitted about the trees.

In the months following Luciano's disappearance, Fabiano had spent more and more time recalling his childhood days, trying to uncover some clue in his father's behavior that would point to what had become of him. Then one day he remembered a particular afternoon in autumn when they had sat together watching harvesters working in the olive groves on the far slope of the mountain. Luciano had been even more silent than usual, and when Fabiano asked if he was all right, Luciano replied by asking if Fabiano ever wondered what it would be like to be another person. Fabiano had found it a strange question, shook his head, and thought no further of it. Recalling it years later, he had dismissed it again and had come to believe that Luciano was gone because he had fallen into some compromising situation, something dark that put his family in danger and that forced him to become another person. It was easier than believing his father had abandoned them. One thing Fabiano knew for sure: wherever Luciano was, he was not with Eva, who had been a girl of eighteen at the time and who had never shown any interest in his middle-aged father.

The church bell ringing the hour of noon across the piazza brought Fabiano back to the present. There was a flight leaving from Naples, the closest international airport, the following afternoon, arriving in New York in the evening. He clicked the link and purchased the ticket.

* * *

Luciano sat in front of Sister Michela's big mahogany desk with his hands in his lap, waiting for her, wondering what she could possibly want to see him about.

The door creaked open, and Luciano rose from his chair as Sister Michela entered and took her place at the desk.

"Good afternoon, Bruno. I hope you're well."

Luciano nodded. "And you, sister?"

"Very well, thank you. I'll get right to the point. I understand two women were here to see you last night. One of them seemed quite agitated."

Luciano turned his gaze to a pen on the sister's desk. "Yes," he said, "she thought she knew me."

"And did she know you?"

"No."

Sister Michela looked at him intently for a few moments. "Bruno, if there's something you need to unburden . . ."

Luciano shook his head. "There's nothing."

"Sister Agnes was at the reception desk last night, and she felt that the women were acting suspiciously and were adamant in their insistence on seeing you."

"It was a misunderstanding, that's all."

"I see. Bruno, do you remember when you first came here?"

"Of course."

"You said you didn't remember who you were. I made inquiries with the police but could find out nothing, and so we never spoke of it again. And you proved to be dedicated and hard-working. We have never had any trouble with you."

Luciano did not try to hide his annoyance. "Excuse me, sister, but why are we discussing this? Why did Sister Agnes feel the need to tell you I had visitors?" He knew the sisters at the Casa looked after him, but now he wondered if Sister Agnes had stuck her nose in where it didn't belong.

Sister Michela looked surprised at his sudden change of tone. "We're discussing this because in all these years you've never come to me to tell me who you really are."

Luciano's mouth went dry, and he hesitated. "You know who I am," he said.

"You told me at the time that you had no memory of who you were, that you had had an accident resulting in a head injury."

Luciano rose from his chair. "If you don't want me to stay here anymore—"

"Sit down."

Luciano sat.

"Bruno, to have one's memory erased so thoroughly and so permanently is an extremely rare condition. It's not a crime to run from an unpleasant life, but running is not a remedy for relieving pains from the past. There's always a way to rectify what seems like an impossible situation. I only ask that you think about it, for your own sake."

Luciano nodded. "Thank you, sister. May I leave now? I have a lot of work to do."

Sister Michela dismissed him and fifteen minutes later he was furiously clipping the hedges at the guest house's front entrance. Instead of being grateful to Sister Michela for not pressing him all these years, Luciano felt betrayed. He always suspected that this clever woman knew he was hiding something, but now she had called him out on it, and he burned with embarrassment. When he had first arrived at the Casa, he was only seeking temporary refuge, terrified of being sent to prison for whatever he had done to Eva Amadeo. But when days turned into weeks, then months, without the police coming for him, Luciano had become complacent. He told himself he would soon be back in Benvenuto, that he just needed a small vacation from the pressures of his daily life and from the demands of a wife who, despite her love and fidelity to him, could never bring herself to fully trust him. Sister Michela allowed him to stay, never questioning him, never pushing. Months turned into years, and Luciano came to love his simple, quiet life at the Casa where there was no need to drink to find peace. He was content here, although sometimes he suffered bouts of melancholy, missing the people he had left behind and wondering why no one who loved him had ever tried to find him.

He often thought of his wife. He remembered the day he had come across her walking the country road outside her grandfather's farm, proud and erect, a long braid hanging down her back. Her dress was orange. He remembered that—a pale orange dress with tiny pink flowers woven into the print. He had tried to seduce her with flattering words and, in his arrogance, thought she would be charmed by them. Instead, he received a crack on the jaw with a metal goat bell. From that moment on he knew he loved her. No shrinking violet was Natalia. She could take care of herself. Perhaps that's why he felt he could leave her for a while, that she would be okay without him.

Chapter 10

May 25

Stella was asleep when Eva retrieved Marcus Aurelius, her black Labrador, from Mrs. O'Connor, who lived upstairs in their house in Forest Hills. The house was on a tree-lined street two blocks from busy Metropolitan Avenue, with its stores and restaurants and the café Eva managed. Mrs. O'Connor had been kind enough to take care of Marcus Aurelius while Eva and Stella were away, but they had arrived home after eleven o'clock the night before and Eva thought it inconsiderate to call on Mrs. O'Connor at so late an hour. She had missed the dog, and Marcus's elated jumping and tail-wagging showed that he had missed her, too.

Now Marcus Aurelius sat quietly at Eva's feet as she sipped her morning coffee in the kitchen, staring out the window at a robin in the backyard and wondering what she should do about Luciano Benini. The more she thought about it, the more she was convinced that the man she had seen in Rome was, indeed, Luciano. And if it was Luciano, then the Luciano she had seen at the bottom of the ravine was not lifeless, only dazed, and that for some mysterious reason he had abandoned his family. She should have been elated when she saw him alive and well, but after the shock and confusion had worn off, all she felt was cheated. She had been carrying the burden of a guilt that was unfounded, and now as she sipped her coffee, the dog's snoring the only sound in the kitchen, her conviction hardened into resentment and anger against Luciano for never returning to Benvenuto.

The sound of a bedroom door opening and the shuffling of feet towards the bathroom told Eva that Stella was awake. Ten minutes later, her hair tousled and eyes barely open, Stella came into the kitchen and poured herself a cup of coffee from the pot on the counter. Marcus thumped his tail at her arrival but remained at Eva's feet.

"Gone halfway across the world and not so much as a bark upon my return," said Stella as she sat at the table across from Eva.

"Do you think I should tell her?"

"Tell who what?"

"Natalia. She has a right to know."

"Eva, I'm barely awake and I have to go to the tailor shop today. Can we talk about this later?"

"I want to talk about it now."

"Never a word until now. Two hours in the airport yesterday, eight and a half hours on the plane, a taxi ride back from the airport last night and never a word. But you want to talk about it now."

"Just because I didn't talk about it doesn't mean I didn't think about it."

"The woman hates you, Eva. Why would you want to talk to her?"

"Because she thinks I ran away with her husband."

"And if you tell her you saw her husband in Rome, do you think she's going to believe you? Don't get involved in this. Let that family work out their own problems."

"How could he not recognize me? I haven't changed that much."

"Maybe he didn't want to recognize you. If he never went back to Benvenuto, he must have his reasons."

"He looked like he genuinely didn't recognize me. Amnesia, maybe? Could the fall have knocked out his memory?"

"For fifteen years? That only happens in the movies, Eva."

"There must be an explanation. And if you were married and your husband left, wouldn't you want to find out where he was?"

"I'd say good riddance."

"No, you wouldn't. You'd want to find out the truth."

Stella lowered her cup and stared at Eva before answering. "Is this really about Natalia, or do you hope to find out more for your own sake and telling Natalia might lead to some answers."

Eva took a long sip of coffee. "Maybe both."

"Think long and hard before you do anything that might make matters worse. Anyway, I'm going to the shop today. I haven't seen my father yet, so I may as well go to work while I'm there." Stella got up from the table and carried her coffee cup out of the room.

Eva stroked the dog's fur with her bare foot as she considered Stella's advice. Her phone lay on the table where she had left it the night before. She reached for it and tapped in her father's number.

Umberto's voice came through calm and comforting. Eva explained how she and Stella had gone to the guest house to see if the man who worked there was Luciano Benini, but Umberto insisted it could not have been him.

"There are many people who look like other people," he said. "Where did you say you met him?"

"The Casa di Santa Rosalia. He's the gardener there."

"Luciano was a grocer, not a gardener."

"We must tell Natalia, papa. Even if there's the slightest possibility that it's him."

"And if it's not him? It would be cruel to give her false hope."

"It was him."

"Eva, I don't want you getting involved in this. There is nothing to be done about it, so put it out of your mind."

"Stella said the same thing."

"Good. Now go back to your life and forget all of this."

Eva thanked her father and ended the call. He and Stella were right. She had no part to play in the affairs of the Benini family. Luciano was alive. She had done no harm to him. He had fallen, that was all, and if he had decided not to return home to his family, well, that was none of her business.

* * *

With Fabiano now on his way to America, Natalia could turn her attention back to the grocery store. She and Liliana were restocking shelves in the late afternoon sun streaming through the store's front window when Liliana slammed a jar of marmalade on the countertop. "I can't believe you're sending him across the ocean on a fool's errand," she said.

Natalia did not respond. As much as she loved her daughter, she often had a hard time understanding her. Liliana had never cried over her father's desertion. She had remained stoic throughout the police questionings, the searches, and the eventual reality that Luciano was not coming home. Natalia, too absorbed in her own grief at the time, later regretted not being more attentive to her.

"What do you hope to accomplish with this?" Liliana asked. "My father is not there, mama. He's not with Eva Amadeo."

"Don't be difficult, Liliana."

"Difficult? You insist with absolutely no proof that you know where he is, and *I'm* being difficult?"

"I do know where he is."

"No, mama, you don't."

"You'll see. Fabiano will find him."

Natalia's conviction that her son would put things right had made her softer that day, less inclined to argue with Liliana, who only shook her head in disgust and continued unboxing the marmalade jars. Natalia was about to open a carton of biscotti when a customer came in. It was Umberto Amadeo.

Liliana looked at her mother. Natalia stood erect and looked hard at Umberto. "What do you want?" she asked. "You're not welcome here."

Umberto came forward and placed a slip of paper on the counter. "You're likely to find your husband working in a guest house in Rome and not philandering in America with my daughter. I took the liberty of looking up the phone number for you."

"You're lying," said Natalia.

"See for yourself. And when you do, then maybe you'll stop spreading lies about my family."

Natalia stared at him, her chin jutting forward. "If this is true, why haven't you told me sooner?"

"Because I didn't know sooner."

"Get out," said Natalia.

After Umberto left the shop, Natalia and Liliana stared at the paper until Liliana picked it up and read the name of the Casa di Santa Rosalia out loud. Natalia snatched the paper from Liliana's hand. "This is a terrible trick," she said. "He wants to get back at me for going to their house that night." She remained quiet for a while. Outside, the muffled sound of children running up the street sounded far off and unreal.

"Give the paper back to me," said Liliana gently.

"No, I'll do it." Natalia walked to the wall phone beside the counter, her stomach in knots. "How could he know this? He's just being spiteful, that's all. This is a game to him."

She dialed the number and a soft voice answered. "Casa di Santa Rosalia. May I help you?"

Natalia's mouth went dry. "I want to speak to Luciano Benini."

"I don't think there is anyone here by that name, but if you wait a moment, I'll check the guest list."

"No, no. He's one of your employees."

"I'm sorry, *signora*, but no one by that name works here."

"Are you sure?"

"Yes, *signora*, I'm very sure."

"Thank you." Natalia replaced the receiver. There was a chair behind the counter and Natalia sat in it, deflated. "He lied to us, Liliana. That bastard of an Amadeo lied to us. May he rot in hell."

* * *

New York City was big. It radiated out from the clustered heart of Manhattan in all directions like a living star, its points extending to the far borders of four other boroughs. As his plane descended towards John F. Kennedy International Airport, Fabiano's gaze remained fixed at the tiny window while the city below grew bigger. The early evening sun burned strong over the endless streets and rooftops of Queens, and to the west, the tall spires of Manhattan glinted across a ribbon of water.

After they landed, Fabiano took a taxi from the airport to his hotel. He had chosen a hotel in midtown Manhattan, the celebrated hub of the city. After moving from the highway and through a tunnel, the taxi emerged into the crowded streets, with the buildings on either side rising up like canyon walls emblazoned with lights. All around him people moved over sidewalks and streets—a pulsing wave of humanity surging and dividing, yet never stopping.

According to his online research, Eva Amadeo was somewhere in the borough he had just left behind. Although his search had not at first yielded much about where he could find her, further digging uncovered that she was the manager of a café in a neighborhood called Forest Hills, which, according to the map on his computer screen was in Queens, across the East River from Manhattan.

The taxi stopped in front of the glass doors of an elegant-looking lobby. Fabiano paid the driver, who muttered a thank-you after retrieving Fabiano's duffle bag from the car's trunk and pulled away without a further word. The check-in clerk was friendlier, and by the time Fabiano had opened the door to his room, he had had enough of people for the day. After taking a long shower, he ordered a dinner of roasted chicken from room service and settled on the bed with his laptop.

Fabiano pulled up the website of the Crystal Café. The café's address and phone number were written in white script against a dark banner. A photo gallery of the café showed a comfortable interior that might have been the model for a French Impressionist painting. The site contained a menu, general information about operating hours, and a contact page. The contact page made him pause. Since he had agreed to find Eva, he had gone over various scenarios in his head about how he would approach her but couldn't decide on which way was best. He could not imagine that any Amadeo would want to hear from a Benini. He wasn't even sure she would remember him. He had known her only casually in Benvenuto, as people often do in small towns, and by the time Eva had left for America he was already living in Florence.

Fabiano leaned back on the bed against the pillows. The pillows were soft, and he was tired. He would go to the café in the morning and speak with her, would apologize on Natalia's behalf for his mother's outrageous accusations. But first he would call and find out when she would be at the café.

Fabiano picked up his phone from the nightstand and tapped in the number from the website.

After three rings a man's voice answered. "Crystal Café."

Fabiano was expecting the voice to be Eva's. He hesitated.

"Hello?" repeated the voice on the other end.

Fabiano spoke some English. He had learned it at the university, but all he managed to say was, "Eva, please."

"Just a minute."

The noise of subdued gaiety pulsed in the background, and then, after a moment, a woman's voice sounded in his ear. Suddenly nervous, he hung up.

Fabiano lay back on the bed. The absurdity of what his mother had asked him to do, of what he had agreed to, passed over him like a chilling shadow. Staring upwards, what he remembered of Eva's face began to form on the white canvas of the ceiling: the cascade of black hair that framed her face and flowed past her shoulders, the large onyx eyes in a porcelain face. Her physical features were all he really knew of Eva Amadeo. Whatever dreams she might have had, whatever deeds she had done, were closed to him.

The ringing of his cell phone recalled Fabiano's attention, and he saw Natalia's number on the small screen. On the nightstand, the red glow of the digital clock gleamed 8:10 p.m. It was after two o'clock in the morning in Benvenuto.

"Mama, is everything all right?"

Natalia's voice was calm and low. "I wanted to make sure you got there safely. I didn't hear from you."

"I'm fine," he said. "I'll call you after I speak to Eva. I have to go now. I'm tired from the flight."

"Just a minute."

"What? What is it?"

"Umberto Amadeo came to the store today."

"Umberto? Why?"

"To tell us that your father is in Rome. To mock us."

Fabiano's heart sank. "If he's in Rome, why am I here?"

"He's not in Rome. I called the number Amadeo gave me at some guest house, and they never heard of him. It was just a ruse."

"You must be mistaken, mama. Or maybe Umberto was mistaken. Why would he tell you something like that knowing it wasn't true?"

"Because that family is vile. I wanted you to know this. I wanted you to know what kind of people you're dealing with when you go to see that woman."

"I'm sorry he upset you, mama. I'll call you as soon as I find out anything. Goodbye."

Fabiano contemplated what his mother had just told him. He couldn't believe that Umberto Amadeo would be so malicious as to purposely mislead her. Natalia's grief had warped her sense of reality where the Amadeos were concerned. She must have misunderstood. Yet why would Umberto think Luciano was in Rome, and what phone number had he given her? He could think of no explanation.

There was a pad and pencil on the nightstand compliments of the hotel. Fabiano turned to his laptop, scribbled down the address of the Crystal Café, and tucked the paper in his wallet. He clicked the link for the contact page on the website and sent a message. It was short and vague. Perhaps she would respond. No matter if she didn't. He did not come all this way just to send an email. Tomorrow he would go to Forest Hills and find Eva. Tonight he would enjoy his roasted chicken, watch a bit of American television, and get a good night's sleep. He turned off his laptop just as a knock on his door and the announcement of "room service" told him his dinner had arrived.

Chapter 11

May 26

Fabiano sat in the back of the taxi as it crawled along Fifth Avenue. They were only blocks from the Metropolitan Museum of Art, the first on his list of places to see while in New York. He had planned to go to the Crystal Café that morning, but when he called the café to find out what hours Eva was working, the girl who answered said that Eva usually worked afternoons and evenings.

"I can leave a message for her," she said. "Who should I say is calling?"

Fabiano had told her not to bother and hung up. He would go back that evening.

Now, as the cab pulled up to the curb, Fabiano thought how magnificent the building was, so majestic and solid, sprawling across the avenue like a reclining white tiger. The fountains that stretched in front sent plumes of white water upwards, penetrating the air with its sound of rushing music. It was a fine set of fountains, worthy of admiration, and the building itself was as beautiful as any in Florence.

Inside was a labyrinth. High-ceilinged, brightly lit rooms lined with paintings led into cozy interiors of elaborate antique furniture and decorative tableware, which further led into corridors of marble statues and ancient stonework. Fabiano took his time rambling across centuries and continents, stopping on the way to drink in the colors of a brilliant brushstroke, examine the setting of a jewel-encrusted goblet, revel in the flow of movement of a dancing nymph. There was a peacefulness here, a kind of soothing tranquility in spite of the numbers of noisy visitors streaming past him in endless repetition. It was as if the artwork itself pulsed with life at a vibration so far above the human that it manifested in a feeling, a delicate web cast over the rooms, over the floors and walls, over the mad, mad world of flesh and blood at its feet.

In front of a collection of silver chalices dating to the Middle Ages, Fabiano caught a glimpse of himself in the exhibit case glass. It was a ghostly image, barely there, as if he were looking at the distilled essence of himself rather than the corporeal man. He looked exhausted, and there was a crease between his eyebrows that had not been there a few days ago when he had watched the sun rising over the Arno, blissfully sipping his coffee.

Down the exhibit corridor the high arches of the rooms ahead pulled him forward. His attention darted from one item to another in this universe of objects as he tried to form a plan for his visit rather than wander aimlessly. He would focus on examining three rooms, he decided, and they would have to be the next three because he could spend all day there if he had the time, but he didn't. He had to go to Forest Hills to talk to Eva.

Passing into the next gallery, he found himself looking up at the large gray eyes of Joan of Arc staring off into a distant dimension. The canvas was vast, a tapestry of muted earth tones pulling him in just as Joan was pulled outward into the divine. Beside him a young couple discussed the saint's calling, wondering if it had been genuine, or if perhaps, instead of heeding the voice of

God and angels, she really had been consorting with demons, as the early authorities had accused her of, or was psychotic, as modern psychiatry might diagnose her. Fabiano had always believed that Joan's summoning was genuine, and looking at the serene face on the canvas, so ready to submit to her divine fate, he envied her. He wished that he, too, could hear the voices of angels, some sign confirming that this ridiculous mission he was on was a genuine one in the eyes of God, one in which he was following the command to "honor thy mother and thy father." He wished this because he knew it was not.

* * *

The Crystal Café was comfortable in its casual elegance. Its walls painted dark green with white trim, it was decorated like a Victorian-era café, with vintage brass chandeliers, stained-glass floor lamps flanking chintz sofas by a large fireplace, and antique prints in ornate frames covering the walls. The café was quiet at this hour, with only a few customers lingering over coffee after having had their lunch. In her office, the afternoon sun pouring onto her shoulders through the window by her desk, Eva stared at her computer screen. She had a lot to catch up on since returning from Italy, but instead of working she sat back in her chair reading a strange email someone had sent through the contact page of the website. It was addressed directly to her and written in Italian: *Hello, Eva. I'm from Benvenuto and would like to visit you here in New York. I will come to the café tomorrow.* There was no signature.

Eva had been in Benvenuto only a few days prior and no one there had made any mention of coming to New York. The message showed it had been written the night before, not long after the phone call she had received. One of the wait staff had answered and called her to the phone, saying only that it sounded like a man's voice. The evening had been busy and the waiter eager to get back to his tables, so he had not thought to ask the caller's name. When Eva answered, the caller hung up. She had not thought much of it at the time, but now, after receiving this message, she wondered if it was the same person.

Eva's phone rang. It was Stella.

"Hello?" Eva could hear Stella's father in the background taking an order from a customer.

"I wanted to let you know that I'll be home a little later than usual this evening so don't worry. There's an opening at the Museum of Art and Design for a new textile exhibit. I should be home around ten."

"Okay," said Eva. "Stella, did anyone in Benvenuto say anything to you about coming to New York?"

"No. I would have mentioned it to you. Why?"

"I got an email today and I don't know what to make of it. Someone saying they're from Benvenuto and wanting to see me. I don't know who it's from."

"That's odd. Maybe the person lived in Benvenuto a long time ago, someone you don't remember, and they live here now."

"Not too many people leave Benvenuto. And why would they want to see me now, anyway?

"Who knows?"

"But why wouldn't the person leave a name?"

"Forgot, maybe? In a hurry? Wants to surprise you?"

"It's just a little disturbing, that's all. Last night someone called the café and hung up when I answered."

"Maybe it's Natalia coming back to haunt you."

"Very funny, Stella."

"Okay, bad joke. I'm sorry. But honestly, Eva, you think too much."

After Stella hung up, Eva went back to staring at the computer screen. Although the message did not require a response, she wrote in Italian, *I would be happy to meet you at the Crystal Café. Please tell me your name.*

When no immediate reply came, she turned to the stack of invoices on her desk.

Chapter 12

Even on a weeknight the Crystal Café was busy. Eva usually enjoyed hearing the low, steady chatter of customers, but tonight she had a headache. After replying to that puzzling email, she had spent the entire afternoon and most of the evening staring at spreadsheets as she worked through the café's invoices. Now, the pain that had been throbbing across her forehead all day had gotten stronger. As she got up to get a cup of coffee, she made a mental note to replenish the empty bottle of aspirin she kept in her desk drawer.

In the kitchen, the staff did not seem to notice her as they worked. She poured the coffee and took the cup into the dining room. Standing by the mantelpiece, Eva surveyed the room. All the customers seemed to be enjoying themselves. Outside the café window, the usual traffic rolled along Metropolitan Avenue, a steady flow of passing cars and pedestrians enjoying the warm spring night. Two young women came in and took a table at the back of the room. A couple walking a small dog stopped to look at the Crystal's menu posted on the door, said a few words to one another, and continued on their way. A young man walked quickly past and then appeared again on the other side of the street, standing there as if waiting for a friend before hurrying off. From where she stood, Eva could not get a good look at his face, but something in his build, in the way he stood, looked familiar. Perhaps he would be back later when his friend showed up.

Eva's head continued to throb. She finished her coffee and went back to her office to get her house keys. After telling one of the servers she was going home for aspirin, she left the soft glowing lights and cheerful sounds of the Crystal behind her and stepped out onto Metropolitan Avenue.

When Eva reached her street and turned the corner, she thought she heard someone walking behind her. Even on a pleasant spring night, the residential streets of this section of Forest Hills were quiet. Perhaps it was one of her neighbors. She stopped and turned around to offer a greeting, but no one was there. A sensation that she was being followed overcame her, and she quickened her pace until she was safely inside her front hallway with Marcus Aurelius there to meet her, his tail wagging.

The house was dark and quiet. Eva drew the curtains in the living room before turning on the lights, then did the same in the kitchen. There was aspirin in the cupboard above the sink, and she swallowed three tablets with a glass of cold tap water. Sitting at the table, she closed her eyes and breathed deeply, grateful for the soothing silence of the room. Marcus sat on the floor next to her and laid his head on her knee. She stroked his neck, the smooth fur soft and comforting against her hand.

Eva was still puzzled by the email she had gotten earlier in the day. After receiving no reply, she had expected the sender to show up at the café. This person— she didn't know if it was a man or a woman—seemed eager to see her, yet nothing followed. Maybe the sender had a change of heart. Maybe—.

Eva's eyes jolted open as Marcus Aurelius jumped up, barking madly, and ran out of the kitchen. She followed and found him at the front door, his barking now turned to growling, his body stiff. Someone was outside the door.

"Who is it?" she called but received no answer. "I have a guard dog," she shouted.

Eva thought she heard retreating footsteps as Marcus continued to growl. He then relaxed and padded into the living room. She followed and found Marcus lying on the carpet before the curtained bay window. After turning out the light, she carefully stepped over him and drew a sliver of curtain away. Outside, the dim white rays of the street lights showed no movement on the block.

* * *

On the corner of the quiet street, Fabiano leaned against a tree, feeling like a criminal in hiding. One word kept running through his mind: stupid, stupid, stupid! Earlier, when the taxi had dropped him off in front of the Crystal Café, he had asked the driver to wait for him. The driver had given him directions to the nearest subway station— a twenty-minute walk—and drove off, leaving Fabiano on Metropolitan Avenue feeling stranded.

Fabiano had intended to go inside and ask to see Eva, but first he had to figure out exactly what to say. The more he thought about it, he realized that a simple apology for his mother's behavior would not be enough. Natalia would prod him, ask how he knew for sure that his father was not with Eva, and he would not be able to lie to her. Yet each time he thought about it, his words sounded more and more preposterous. *Eva, I'm here to prove to my mother that you did not run away with my father. Eva, I know my father is not here, but I promised my mother I would talk with you anyway and I traveled across an ocean to do so.* He sounded like an imbecile. As he was deciding on what to say, Eva walked out of the café.

The sight of her stepping onto the street so unexpectedly alarmed him, and he questioned yet again why he had agreed to do this. Her face was fleeting as she turned, but Fabiano could clearly see the lines of her profile fading into shadow as she walked away. Eva Amadeo had not changed all that much in fifteen years.

Like a fool he began to follow her. As she turned around, he darted into the closest driveway and concealed himself in the shadows of a house. It was a cowardly move, but he didn't want her to think he was a stalker. She continued on her way, faster now, and he watched her from the edge of the yard until she hurried up the front porch steps of a two-story house and went inside. He followed and got as far as the front lawn of the house. After pacing about on the sidewalk, he went up to the front door and was about to ring the doorbell when the loud growling of a vicious dog stopped him. Eva's voice shouting a warning from behind the door that she had an attack dog was even more threatening than the growling, so Fabiano turned and left.

Now, from his place against the tree, he could see down the block to the yellow glow filtering through the curtains of a downstairs window in Eva's house. He would try again tomorrow. He would go to the café in the afternoon, in the daylight, far from the dog and from the possibility that Eva might accuse him of any menacing behavior.

He turned and walked in the direction of the subway station and the train that would take him back to Manhattan.

* * *

It was almost ten o'clock when Eva, lying on the sofa watching television, heard Stella's key in the front door lock. Eva lowered the volume and Marcus Aurelius thumped his tail on the carpet as Stella came into the living room.

"How was the exhibit opening?" Eva asked.

"The wine was good, but the textiles were not. The colors were too garish on most of them." Stella patted Marcus on the head, then sat in the lounge chair opposite Eva. "I hate to sound immodest," she said, "but my designs are so much nicer. It seemed like these were—. Are you okay? Why are you not at work?"

"Headache."

"That's not usually enough to keep you from the café."

"I came home for aspirin but then decided to take the rest of the night off."

"Headache that bad?"

Eva sat up, facing her cousin. "It wasn't the headache. I didn't want to go out again. When I was walking home, I felt like someone was following me, but I couldn't see anyone. Then after I got home, someone came up to the front door but left before ringing the bell. Marcus went crazy."

Stella frowned. "That's strange. Maybe somebody just had the wrong house."

"Maybe. But it was very disturbing."

"I wouldn't worry about it. It's just your nerves. You've been knee-deep in drama these past few days. Any news from the person who emailed you?"

Eva shook her head. "Not a word. And nobody came to see me today."

"Well, I suppose they got caught up doing something else and couldn't make it. Maybe you'll hear from them tomorrow."

"How can you always be so calm about everything?"

"What's not to be calm about? Do you think someone is out to hurt you?"

Eva sighed. "Probably not. It's just creepy, that's all. First the mysterious email, now the mysterious caller at the door. What if it's the same person?"

"If it is, then this person is not very good at making contact. Listen, things will look a lot better in the daylight." Stella patted Eva on the head. "I have an early day tomorrow so I'm going to bed. I'm glad your headache is better."

"Did I say it was?" Eva said to Stella's retreating back.

Eva turned the television off and lay back down. She would sleep on the sofa that night, with Marcus on the floor beside her, and she would leave the lights on.

Chapter 13

May 27

Fabiano had arrived at the café too early. When he asked the waitress if he could speak to Eva Amadeo, the girl said that Eva had not come in yet. So Fabiano took a seat at a table near the door and ordered a cup of coffee. Now, three cups later, he wondered if Eva would ever show up. He wanted to get this over with, to have a short conversation with her so that he could go back to Manhattan and continue his day. He would take a long walk through Central Park, visit a few art galleries in Soho, and maybe take in a Broadway show if he could get a ticket on such short notice. There was so much he wanted to see and do, and now that he was in New York, he was almost glad that Natalia had sent him on this pointless errand.

Fabiano was bored. He had already played six games of solitaire on his phone while he waited, scrolled through the latest news, and was about to text Liliana to find out what was going on back home when the door opened and in walked Eva. She sailed through the dining room without a passing glance and disappeared into a back room. Fabiano looked around for the waitress. She was taking an order from an elderly couple, her back to him.

When she turned to go to the kitchen, he signaled her over to his table.

"More coffee?" she asked.

"No, thank you. I want to speak to Eva Amadeo."

The waitress looked like she had suddenly remembered something. "Oh, right! Sorry. I got so busy I forgot."

She poked her head into the back room and a moment later Eva was walking towards him. Eva looked serious, almost anxious. He stood up as she approached him, and she said nothing when she reached the table, as if expecting him to take the lead. Fabiano found it strange that she did not even say so much as *Can I help you?* or *I understand you wanted to see me*, but the look on her face was almost an explanation. She seemed reluctant to approach him, and for one mad instant he wondered if perhaps his mother had been right all along and he would find his father here in Forest Hills, here in Eva's world, in Eva's life, and then what would he do? But the thought was fleeting, and he greeted her with a smile.

"Good afternoon," he said. "Please sit down."

Eva sat opposite him, straight-backed and stiff. Still she did not smile.

* * *

As soon as Eva saw him from across the room, she knew who he was. The shock of recognition caused her to almost turn away and hurry back to her office. So this was the mysterious stranger who had sent the email. What could Fabiano Benini possibly want with her?

Eva walked towards him, trying not to pay attention to the familiar clenching of her stomach that happened whenever she encountered the threat of a Benini. She noticed Fabiano had gotten up from the table as she approached him—a polite thing to do. This gesture and the benign, almost apologetic, look on his face told her he was probably not there to cause trouble. She accepted his offer to join him at the table and motioned for him to sit.

"Do you remember me?" he asked. "Fabiano Benini?"

She nodded.

"I'm glad you agreed to see me," he said.

"The waitress just said someone wanted to speak to me. I had no idea it was you."

Fabiano lowered his eyes and ran his finger over the rim of his coffee cup. "I . . ." He took a deep breath. "I know my mother came to your parents' house recently."

Eva should have asked him what he, the son of a man who had left his family and a mother who blamed her for this fact, was doing in her café in Queens on a weekday afternoon as if he were just another customer. Instead, she allowed him to continue.

"Eva, I want to apologize for my mother's behavior. She shouldn't have done what she did."

Eva was caught off guard. Although she didn't know what to expect from this meeting, she certainly did not expect this. "You want to apologize for your mother's behavior? So you don't think I bewitched your father into running away with me?"

Fabiano smiled. "No, I don't. I don't think anyone except my mother thinks that."

Eva sat back in her chair in disbelief. For a moment she just stared at Fabiano, who stared back. "And you came all the way from Italy to tell me this?"

"No . . . no, I was . . . I was coming anyway. I'm here on vacation." He began to play with his coffee cup again, running his finger over the handle this time.

Eva was amused by his sudden discomfort. He was hiding something, but it was not something insidious. He was telling an innocent fib. "It's quite a coincidence, you coming here so soon after your mother's outburst," she said.

"Well . . . my vacation may have coincided with something my mother wanted me to do."

"And that is . . .?"

"Make sure my father wasn't here."

Eva stiffened. So he *was* here to snoop and accuse. "He is not," she said.

Fabiano's expression quickly changed to concern. "I know that. I never expected him to be. I just want to be able to tell my mother that I saw you and spoke to you, to finally put an end to this crazy delusion she has about you. That's the truth, I swear it."

Eva eyed him suspiciously. "I live with my cousin in a house a few blocks from here. Do you want to come and see for yourself? I assure you, you will find no trace of your father, or of any man, living there."

Fabiano shook his head. "That's not necessary. I don't know where my father's been all these years, but wherever he is, he obviously wants nothing to do with his family. I can't convince my mother of that, though, so if it takes a trip across the Atlantic to get her to believe it, the time and expense is worth it. I know if I tell her my father's not here, she'll believe me."

"And what makes you think that?"

"Because she trusts me."

Eva paused to take all of this in. Here was a Benini apologizing. Here was a Benini saying he believed in her innocence. Here was a Benini saying he would put things right with his family so that Natalia would finally leave the Amadeos alone and perhaps even feel some remorse for the slanderous allegations she had heaped on Eva's reputation.

"I have to tell you something," she said. "Something I just found out." Eva struggled to find the right words as Fabiano waited patiently. "I think I know where you can find your father."

* * *

In Benvenuto the townspeople were enjoying their evening *passeggiata* when Natalia locked up the grocery store and stepped out into the street with Liliana. The town always looked best in the early evening. She liked the way the waning sunlight reflected off the walls and winding stone streets. It calmed her nerves whenever she suffered through a bad day, and these past two days, since Umberto Amadeo had visited her shop, had been particularly bad.

Natalia still stewed over his audacity. Sweeping the shop's floor or tidying up the countertop, she would remember how he had come in and blatantly lied to her and Liliana, and she would be overtaken with a desire for revenge. He had given her a grain of hope, and when she had accepted that grain like a hungry child, it had been snatched from her hand and crushed underfoot. Liliana had told her that she must let it go for the sake of her sanity and physical health, but she could not. She was as sick as when Eva Amadeo had first shown up, and if it were not for Liliana's threats of leaving her in the shop to fend for herself, she would have remained home in bed until Fabiano returned.

Natalia and Liliana walked down the street and entered the piazza. It was alive with people strolling and chatting, children playing, and old people on benches taking it all in.

"I'm thinking of going to the market at Santa Chiara tomorrow," said Liliana as they crossed the piazza. "I need to buy a few things. Would you mind if I left the shop for a couple of hours?"

"Of course not."

"Maybe you want to come with me? Uncle Maurizio is always willing to take over for us if we need him."

Natalia stopped abruptly. Sitting on the edge of the fountain, smoking a pipe and looking like he didn't have a care in the world, was Umberto Amadeo.

"Oh, no," said Liliana.

Natalia stormed over to the fountain with Liliana trailing behind. She began addressing Umberto even before she reached him. "How dare you, Amadeo? How dare you lie to me?"

Umberto frowned as the two women approached. He looked at Natalia as if she had lost her senses. "What are you talking about now?"

"Mama," said Liliana, "please don't."

Natalia was now inches from Umberto. "They never heard of him," she said. "He was never there."

Umberto looked puzzled. "If you mean Luciano, I only told you what I heard."

"Heard from where? How could you know such a thing?" People around them were staring, but Natalia didn't care. "You're a liar, Umberto Amadeo, a liar like the rest of your miserable family."

Umberto hopped off the fountain and hovered over Natalia. "You keep my family out of this, you stupid woman. There's something wrong with you up here." He struck his temple with his index finger several times, putting his face closer to hers.

"Mama, please," Liliana pleaded. "Don't do this again. Let's go home."

Liliana pulled at her mother's arm, but Natalia's anger had overtaken her. "I want to know how you could be such a bastard," she shouted. "Why did you do this to me? To my daughter? Were you trying to punish me for coming to your house to confront your good-for-nothing daughter for what she did to me and my family?"

Umberto's nostrils flared. Several people had gathered closer and seemed about to intervene when Umberto, his jaw clenched, turned and walked away, muttering swears at Natalia.

Natalia tried to follow but Liliana held her back. "That's right, walk away!" she shouted after him. "You have nothing to say to me, is that right?"

"Mama, why do you always do this?" There was mortification in Liliana's voice as she shepherded her mother out of the piazza and onto the street that led to their home.

* * *

Eva's words felt like a physical slap across Fabiano's face. "How could you possibly know where my father is?"

"Because I saw him," she said. "After I left Benvenuto, I went to Rome and I saw him there. He works as a gardener in a convent guest house. He didn't seem to know who I was and said he had never been to Benvenuto, but I'm sure it was him."

Fabiano's face burned. "Stop right there," he said. He was hearing the same lie Umberto had told Natalia the day before. He realized now that Natalia had not misunderstood. Eva may have been innocent of what Natalia accused her of, but she was not innocent in this. She was spiteful and manipulative like her father.

"I know this must be a shock," said Eva, "but—"

"How can you do this?"

Eva looked bewildered. "What do you mean?"

"How can you make up a story like that?"

Her eyes widened. "It's not a story."

"Your father went to my family's store yesterday and upset my mother with the same lie."

"My father? My father spoke to your mother about this?"

"What is wrong with your family?"

"I'm telling you the truth. Why don't you believe me?"

"Because my mother called this guest house. Your father gave her the phone number, but when she called, they said they never heard of him."

Eva looked genuinely confused. "I don't understand," she said. "Why would the sisters at the guest house say he wasn't there?"

"Maybe because he wasn't?"

Fabiano was about to get up and leave when Eva seemed to suddenly remember something. "Who did your mother ask for?" she asked.

"What?"

"Did she ask for Luciano? Because he uses another name now. Bruno. They know him there as Bruno."

"Then why didn't your father tell my mother to ask for Bruno?"

"Because he didn't know."

"How convenient."

"No, really. I don't think I ever mentioned that name to my father. I just told him that I saw Luciano."

Fabiano held up a hand to stop Eva from talking. His head was spinning, and he didn't know what to believe. His mother only said that Umberto Amadeo had come into the store and told her that she could find Luciano at a certain place in Rome. Umberto probably had not stayed long after that. Fabiano wished he had asked his mother for more details. Suddenly he felt nauseous. "I have to go," he said, rising abruptly. He pulled some bills out of his wallet, threw them on the table, and hurried out of the Crystal Café.

* * *

After Fabiano Benini left the Crystal in a flustered hurry, Eva ignored the curious stares of the waitress and the café diners and went back to her office, closing the door behind her. She paced the room, then grabbed her phone from its place on her desk and tapped in her father's number. It went straight to voicemail. "Call me," she said, "It's important."

Slipping the phone into her pocket, she went back into the dining room, and after pouring herself a glass of Merlot, walked out into the street, glass in hand, and called Stella.

"It was him," she said when Stella answered the phone.

"Who? What? You just jump into conversation lately, Eva, and I have no idea what you're talking about."

"The person who emailed me. It was Fabiano Benini. He came to see me today at the café."

"Whoa! Stop! Are you kidding me?"

Eva told Stella all that had happened with Fabiano, and when she finished, Stella calmly replied, "Well, at least you know who it is now."

"Really? Is that all you can say?"

"I don't know what else to say. What kind of an idiot would travel across an ocean to satisfy some weird quirk of his mother's imagination? It sounds creepy to me. Was he the one outside our house the other night when Marcus went into conniptions?"

"I hadn't even thought of that."

"Well, just be careful. He might come back for revenge."

"He's not a maniac, Stella."

"You don't know that. He might take after his mother."

Eva's phone buzzed with an incoming call. "I have to go. My father's calling."

Stella hung up and the next thing Eva heard was Umberto's voice sounding concerned.

"Your message said it was important. Is anything wrong?"

"No. I just want to know why you went to see Natalia Benini after you told me not to contact her."

"How do you know about that?"

"Just answer me."

"I didn't want you to get involved. You don't need the aggravation. Now tell me how you know I spoke to Natalia Benini."

"Because her son was here today."

There was silence on the other end.

"Did you hear what I said, papa? Fabiano Benini came to my café to speak to me. But before I tell you what happened, tell me this: did I ever mention that Luciano was now going by the name Bruno?"

"No, Eva, you did not."

"Then you didn't tell Natalia to ask for Bruno when she called the guest house?"

"No, of course not. No wonder she said they never heard of him." Umberto sounded exasperated.

"Oh, papa, you have to tell her."

"I just saw her not a half hour ago in the piazza. She was livid. She called me a liar and insulted our family. Eva, how could you leave out a detail as important as that?"

"Because when I told you about it, I had just seen someone I thought was dead. I'm sorry if I was too upset to remember that he uses another name. And why are you getting annoyed with me? I didn't know you were going to tell Natalia. You said we should leave it alone."

Umberto's hard breathing came across the line. "Tell me about the son. What was he doing in your café? Did he threaten you?"

"No, it wasn't like that." Eva repeated what she had described to Stella, only this time fielding interruptions from her father who insisted on asking questions before she had a chance to finish her story. When she was through, Umberto made her promise to call the police if Fabiano showed up again.

"He was harmless, papa. And I don't think he'll be coming back. Now please, since you already gave Natalia the phone number of the guest house, you have to let her know that Luciano is using a different name. Her son didn't believe me. Maybe she'll believe you."

* * *

There was a park not far from the Crystal Café. Fabiano could see it ahead as he hurried along Metropolitan Avenue. It looked vast and forested, and all he wanted to do was get lost in it. A pathway bordered on either side by trees and thick vegetation led Fabiano into the park's interior. He was hidden here, where he could be alone with his thoughts.

Walking slowly along one of the many paths meandering through the towering trees, Fabiano's anxiety began to dissolve. The exercise and the fresh air helped to clear his head, and he wondered if maybe he had been too hasty in condemning Eva. Were the Amadeos really capable of being such monsters? He doubted it. This was all probably just a big, unpleasant misunderstanding. But truth or not, misunderstanding or not, he had to find out for himself if his father was in Rome.

Fabiano pulled his phone out of his pocket to call his mother. He would tell her that his father was not with Eva. He would *not* tell her that Luciano might be living in Rome under another name, not until he was sure Eva was not lying or that she was mistaken in believing the man she had seen was Luciano. Fabiano would go to Rome as soon as he could get a return flight to Italy. His vacation plans would have to wait for another time.

* * *

The phone was ringing on the small table in the foyer as Natalia and Liliana entered the house.

"I don't want to talk to anyone now," Natalia barked as she stormed up the stairs.

Halfway up she heard Liliana on the phone asking about Eva Amadeo and knew it was Fabiano calling.

Natalia came back down. "Give me the phone," she said. She could tell from Liliana's face that the news was not good. Taking the phone from her daughter, and without saying hello, she asked Fabiano if he had met with Eva.

"I have," he said. "And mama, he's not here."

Natalia's chest hurt, as if an invisible hand had reached in and crushed what was left of her heart. "You're sure of that?"

"Yes."

"How do you know?"

"She told me."

Natalia's anger flared. "And you just took her word for it?"

Fabiano's deep sigh was audible on the other end of the line. "Please, mama, let this go."

"She's hiding something. Something is not right." Natalia's voice was rising. Liliana tried to take the phone from her, but she pushed back. "He has to be there. Where else could he be?"

"I'll leave here as soon as I can get a flight home. I'll come to Benvenuto to see you before I go back to Florence."

"You can't come back yet! You have to find him."

"I'm sorry, mama. I'll see you soon."

Fabiano hung up, leaving Natalia in a stupor.

Chapter 14

After speaking to Stella and her father, Eva returned to her office only to find that she could not concentrate on her work, so she decided to clear her head by taking Marcus Aurelius for a walk. Being able to walk the dog during afternoons was one of the benefits of working only a few blocks from home. Eva was grateful for this distraction as Marcus scurried from one spot of curbside grass to another in front of their house.

Marcus never growled at strangers as long as they kept clear of his house and yard, so Eva didn't notice Fabiano coming up behind her until he was almost upon her. Marcus, far from showing any signs of hostility, wagged his tail and strained to sniff Fabiano's clothes as Eva pulled on his leash.

"What are you doing here?" she said as Fabiano backed away from Marcus's nose.

"Please, I just want to talk to you."

"How did you know where to find me? Did you follow me here?"

"I went to the café, and they told me you had stepped out for a while."

"So how did you know where to find me?" she repeated. "Have you been following me?" Eva struggled to keep her anger under control. She had had enough of the Beninis.

"I asked the waitress."

"No one at the Crystal would have told you where I live. They don't give out personal information. Do you think I'm stupid?"

"Of course not. I—"

"My dog will teach you a lesson if you try anything."

Marcus had selected a tree and was busy relieving himself. No longer afraid of the dog, Fabiano smirked, which made Eva even angrier.

"What do you want from me?" she asked. "Why can't you and your mother just leave me alone?"

"I'm sorry, Eva. I shouldn't have run off the way I did earlier. Can we start again?"

"Again for what?"

"You said you saw my father."

"Yes, and you called me a liar."

"Can I at least explain why?"

Eva stood with feet apart staring hard at Fabiano, while Marcus Aurelius, happily relieved, panted beside her. "You still haven't explained how you know where I live."

Fabiano looked down at his feet and hesitated. "I saw you leave the café last night."

"And you followed me? You were spying on me?" Eva's voice was rising now, and she didn't care how loud it got. "So that was you on the porch?"

Fabiano nodded.

"Why did you run away?"

He nodded towards the dog. "That animal sounded like he was going to eat me alive."

"You pathetic coward! You'd rather frighten a woman in her own home?"

"I'm sorry. Really, really sorry. I didn't even know what to say to you. Can we please go somewhere and talk?"

Eva looked down at Marcus and patted him on the head. She waited just to see Fabiano squirm before answering. "Come in the house," she said. "And keep this in mind: this dog *will* eat you alive if I command him to."

Eva led the way up the front porch and unlocked the door. "Go into the living room," she said as they entered. She removed Marcus's leash and hung it on a hook by the door, then joined Fabiano, who stood in the middle of the living room looking uncomfortable. "Sit down," she said, nodding towards the sofa. Fabiano sat and Eva joined him. "Now, say what you have to say."

"Okay, well . . . you have to understand that what you told me today was shocking. And when my mother said that your father had been to see her and that the guest house said he wasn't there, naturally we assumed it was some sort of a hoax."

"Naturally? You automatically assumed that my family and I are that horrible?"

"I wasn't thinking straight."

"Well, I called my father and told him to tell your mother about the name change."

Fabiano looked skeptical. "I doubt she'll believe him."

"Why? Because we're a family of liars?"

"Because she's been gravely disappointed and probably not ready to trust him again."

"Then why don't you call and tell her?"

Fabiano hesitated. "I'd rather not," he said.

Eva got up from the sofa. "Get out."

"Why? What did I do now?"

"You still don't believe me, so get out of my house and leave me and my family alone."

"I do believe you, Eva. I'm going to Rome myself to find him and bring him home." Fabiano got up from the sofa. "I'm leaving now. I said what I had to say."

"Wait." Eva put a hand on his arm as he turned to go. "I'm sorry, okay? This has all been very upsetting for me. Take my phone number and when you find him, let me know how it turns out."

Fabiano pulled his phone from his pocket and added Eva's number. Eva took the hand he offered and shook it, then walked Fabiano to the door.

* * *

The sun setting behind the mountain sent a suffused glow into the sky. Twilight was coming, and as the sky deepened into darkness, so did Natalia. When Fabiano had told her he was coming home, she had stood motionless in the foyer and only moved when Liliana came in to check on her. She barely heard Liliana's words of sympathy as she went upstairs to her bedroom.

Natalia lay down on her bed, face up, still in her street clothes, and let the tears flow. Only one other time had she felt such despair, and that was when Luciano had first disappeared. Yet there had been hope then, at least until it became clear that he was not coming back, and then Natalia's grief threatened to overwhelm her. She had tried to make sense of it at the time and had concluded that Eva Amadeo was the reason why Luciano had left her. Even though she was devastated, at least she had an explanation. Now, with that belief shattered, it was like reliving those first few days of uncertainty. Natalia was sputtering and sinking, with no foothold to save her.

When the doorbell rang, Natalia was too miserable to care. Whoever it was could come back later. She did not expect to hear Umberto Amadeo's voice, muffled by her closed bedroom door, coming up from the foyer mingled with Liliana's surprised and angry response. Umberto tried to speak over Liliana, insisting that he needed to see Natalia, but Liliana held him at bay. The next thing Natalia heard was the front door slamming, cutting off Umberto and his lies.

A few moments later there was a soft knock on her bedroom door. "Come in," she said.

"Mama, Umberto Amadeo wanted to speak to you, but I didn't think it was a good idea. I sent him away."

"Good."

"He said he had something important to tell you, something about papa. Maybe I should have listened."

"No, I don't want to hear anything more from that man or that family. You did the right thing." Natalia held out a limp hand and Liliana took it. "I don't always give you the credit you deserve, Liliana, but let me tell you now, you're a good daughter."

Liliana squeezed her mother's hand. "Can I get you anything?"

"No, thank you. I just need to rest. Please close the door on your way out."

Alone in her room, Natalia wondered what she was going to do next.

* * *

The wet cobblestones of the Piazza Navona glinted in the light of the streetlamps as Luciano headed back to the Casa di Santa Rosalia. It had rained earlier, and Luciano, taking a long walk through the streets of Rome, had found refuge in a small café in a side street off the piazza. He needed to clear his head, and sometimes the calmness of his garden was not enough. Sometimes he needed a long, long walk. This night's walk had taken him over the Tiber.

It had been four days since Eva and her cousin had come to the guest house, four days during which Luciano, triggered by the sight of this girl from his past, had time to remember what he had left behind—his wife and children, his business, his home. For four days he had wrestled with his conscience and questioned the decision he had made long ago to step away from everything, a decision which was supposed to be temporary, but which had solidified into a permanent new life. Luciano didn't even have any photographs of this earlier life, his real life. All he had to rely on were memories, and even those he had pushed to the back of his mind as time went on and he settled into being Bruno, the gardener at the Casa di Santa Rosalia. In the days following his fall, Luciano had thought of his family often, knowing he would soon return to them. But those thoughts became fewer and fewer as time rolled on until the memories, when he did entertain them, only brought pangs of remorse. He had stayed away too long.

As Luciano crossed over the St. Angelo Bridge, he was struck once again by the beauty of the Castel Sant'Angelo, solid and immense, in front of him. He had seen it countless times, yet the sight never grew old for him—the rounded façade behind its imposing wall, the entire structure bathed in a golden glow cast from the electric lights that transformed the Tiber into a shimmering silken cloak. This was only one of the many remarkably beautiful sights of Rome, unrivaled by anything his small town of Benvenuto could offer. He sometimes wondered if the city itself had cast a spell on him that kept him rooted there.

It was late when Luciano returned to his room. He had left his cell phone on the nightstand. It was irresponsible of him because the only time anyone from the Casa called was if there was an emergency. It was not even his phone. It was a work phone given to him by Sister Michela when he had first come to the Casa, and no one but the sisters had the number. Luciano stared at it for a long time. What would happen if he called home? What sounds would he hear in that house so far away in time and place? Would his daughter answer? Would her voice have changed to reflect the mature young woman she must have become? He knew his son was in Florence, but did Fabiano visit his mother and sister often, a man among women to care for them in Luciano's absence, to do the job that Luciano was supposed to do? Or would Natalia pick up the phone, her voice tinged with worry to receive a call so late at night? He closed his eyes and concentrated on recalling the details of his wife's face—the bright eyes, the soft skin, how she often swept her hair up using combs to keep it in place.

Luciano opened his eyes and reached for the phone, his heart pounding. The number to the phone on the little table in the foyer of his house was something he had never forgotten. For what seemed like hours he stared at the phone in his hand, although it could not have been more than minutes as he tried to get his breathing under control. He had no idea what he would say, but the pull to hear those once familiar voices overwhelmed him. Luciano felt as if his blood vessels would burst, and he would drown in his own blood.

He tapped in the numbers and waited. Ring after ring sounded in his ear. Just as he was about to hang up, a sleepy voice answered.

"Hello?"

It was his daughter, Liliana.

"Hello?" she repeated. "Who is this?"

Luciano's throat closed. He barely breathed.

The next thing he heard was the click of the receiver as Liliana hung up, cutting him off from his house and his life in Benvenuto.

Chapter 15

May 30

Fabiano awakened to the sound of traffic in the street below his hotel window. He had wanted to stay at a *pensione* in one of the side streets of Rome where it was quieter and less expensive, but all he could get when he arrived late the night before was a hotel in a busier part of the city. After his last meeting with Eva Amadeo, Fabiano had booked the earliest available flight to Rome, which left him a couple of days to explore New York City. He chose to visit a few of the larger museums but could not enjoy browsing the galleries. Every hour in New York was an hour delayed in Rome.

After showering and dressing, Fabiano went down to the hotel restaurant to have a quick coffee, then headed out to the street. In his hand was the address of the Casa di Santa Rosalia and on his phone was a map that showed its location.

The bright sunshine of the early morning helped to calm his flustered nerves as he made his way to his father, if indeed that's what he would find at the guest house. He tried not to think, hoping that the words he needed to approach the man would come when the moment arrived.

The Casa di Santa Rosalia looked deceptively small from the outside, but when Fabiano stepped through the doors, he found that its interior extended deep into the recesses of a sanctuary designed for contemplation. There was nobody at the reception desk and no one in the lobby. To the side of the entranceway, past the reception desk, a set of French doors led to a garden. His heart beating wildly, Fabiano waited at the desk until clicking heels on the terracotta floor brought a young sister with a bright fresh smile. When Fabiano asked if a man named Bruno worked there, the sister looked at him quizzically.

"Are you a friend?" she asked as she slipped behind the reception desk.

"A relative."

The sister looked surprised as she picked up the desk phone and dialed a number. "He's not answering," she said. "You can try the garden if you like. That's usually where he is this time of the morning." She pointed to the French doors.

Fabiano thanked her and, without a thought or hesitation, walked to the doors and stepped through.

The garden was a wide, neatly tended square of grass bordered by beds of colorful flowers and trees. A marble fountain stood in the center, and beside the fountain was a man bending down as if picking something up from the grass. As Fabiano got closer, the man straightened up.

A flame seared Fabiano's chest. This man, his father, didn't seem to notice him as he placed a set of keys in his pocket, but when he turned in Fabiano's direction, Luciano froze.

Fabiano groped for a nearby bench and sat down, not taking his gaze from his father.

It seemed as if an eternity had passed before Luciano came forward and stood hesitantly over his son. When he sat on the bench beside Fabiano and reached to embrace him, Fabiano pushed him away. Overcome with a swirling blend of emotions—anger, relief, fear of being rejected again, and a pure filial love in spite of it all—Fabiano struggled to keep from crying.

"So, you're really here, then." Fabiano's tone was edged with bitterness, his words clipped as he fought to keep his composure.

Luciano nodded but said nothing.

"And have you been here all this time?"

Luciano nodded again. He looked miserable.

"Why are you here, papa?"

Luciano did not respond, just licked his lips and folded his hands in his lap.

"Answer me!"

Breathing deeply, Luciano remained silent for several moments as Fabiano glared at him. "It's difficult to explain," he said finally, his voice low and measured. "I didn't intend to stay away, Fabi. When I came to Rome, I was desperate."

"Why? Did you do something? Were you in some kind of trouble?"

Luciano seemed to struggle to find the right words to tell what had happened to him since leaving Benvenuto. His voice was strained, his tone remorseful. Fabiano listened silently, his mouth rigid, incredulous that Eva Amadeo—once again at the heart of his family's troubles—had been with his father on the night of the feast.

Luciano described what he could remember of that night, how he had been drunk when he came across Eva out in the countryside, and how, after speaking to her, he had slid down into the ravine and awakened alone in the moonlight with her blood-stained shawl on the ground close by. Fabiano softened when Luciano told of his head injury and explained how he had fled to Rome in a panic, not knowing whether or not he had harmed Eva. But his sympathy ended when Luciano could give no good reason for why he had remained away all these years, leaving those who loved him to worry and to mourn.

"The time passed so quickly," said Luciano, "and so much of it. I thought all of you would hate me because I never contacted you. I thought I would not be welcomed home."

Fabiano shook his head in disgust. "You didn't even try."

"I'm sorry, Fabi. I really am. Your father is a coward."

"Well, Eva Amadeo is alive and well and never suffered any injuries that night, so all this time was wasted. Wasted!"

Luciano looked deflated. He opened his mouth to say something, then closed it.

"Say what you have to say, papa."

"No, it's not important anymore."

"Say it."

"Okay, then. Why did you never come looking for me, you or your mother?"

Fabiano's eyes widened in disbelief. "We did look for you! We had search parties, and we had the police looking, but you had vanished. Why would we even think to look in Rome?"

Both men sat silently for a long while, not looking at one another.

Fabiano stared at the play of light on the water spouting in the fountain. His head reeled. He wanted this meeting to end. He wanted his father back in Benvenuto, in his mother's house, and himself back in Florence, in his apartment overlooking the Arno. "Come back now," he said.

Luciano looked away towards the lemon trees.

"Come home with me. Mama has never been the same since you left. She'll forgive you."

Luciano turned slowly to face his son, his expression sad and resigned.

"Papa?"

"I need a little more time."

Fabiano frowned and shook his head to clear it. "What are you talking about?"

"I need more time, Fabi."

Fabiano shot up from the bench and began to pace. "I don't believe what I'm hearing."

"They know me as another person here, as Bruno Fiorentino. The sisters have been kind to me. I have a job here. I can't just pick up and leave. How would I explain that?"

"How about telling them the truth?"

"It's not a simple thing to swap one life for another so abruptly."

"You've done it before!"

"Fabi . . . please. Try to understand."

Fabiano looked up to the sky and muttered a curse. He turned to his father and said in low, steady tones, "If you don't come home with me now, don't bother to ever come back."

Luciano looked stunned. When he didn't respond, Fabiano stormed off towards the French doors. Once inside the reception area, he ignored the sister at the desk who asked him if everything was all right and walked out onto the street.

Rome was alive with people moving about in the hot sunshine, but Fabiano passed them all without a glance. Head down, body bent forward, he hurried on until he reached his hotel. As he entered the lobby, the concierge offered a friendly greeting. Fabiano grunted a reply, then sprinted up the stairs to his room. He pulled his duffle bag from the floor, threw it on the bed, and began to hastily pack.

Chapter 16

The night sky above Natalia's house was scattered with stars. They seemed to whirl in the sky as she stumbled through the back door and looked up, one hand clinging to the door jamb to steady herself, breathing in as much air as her lungs could take. She felt nauseous, and her breaths came quickly. It was true. Luciano had been found.

Fabiano came up behind her. He placed his arm around her shoulder and gently led her back inside and into the living room, where Liliana stood, her face blank. He had explained everything to them.

"Do you want something to drink?" he asked Natalia as he helped her onto the sofa.

She waved a hand in dismissal.

He turned to his sister. "Do you?"

Liliana shook her head and sat in an armchair.

Fabiano began to pace the floor. Natalia had never seen him so agitated, her son who was usually composed and even-tempered.

"And Eva was with him that night," he said. "She was the cause of all this, yet she said nothing to any of us. Not then and not now."

"You see?" said Natalia. "Neither of you believed me when I told you she was no good. I've always known there was something evil about that family. Watching us suffer like that and not saying a word. They all must have known. They must have!"

"We'll confront them later," said Fabiano, "after we've calmed down."

"And your father? What do we do about him?"

Fabiano stopped pacing and sat beside his mother. "We can't do anything about him. He has to come home when he's ready. We can't force him."

"I don't understand," said Liliana. "Why won't he come back?"

"I told you. He said he needs more time to take care of things."

"He's had fifteen years," said Natalia. "We'll see what he needs to take care of. I'll go to Rome myself and let him tell me to my face."

"No," said Fabiano, "absolutely not. That will only upset you. Just let it be, mama."

"Fabiano is right," said Liliana. "That's not a good idea."

Natalia hesitated, weighing their words. Perhaps they were right. Perhaps she should stop tormenting herself over a husband who had caused her so much grief. She stood up wearily. "I don't have the energy to discuss this anymore. I'm going to bed." She kissed them both goodnight and went upstairs.

But Natalia couldn't sleep. She lay in bed staring at the ceiling, her thoughts boiling. When she did manage to fall into a fitful sleep, she awoke startled and confused until she remembered where she was. The clock on her nightstand read 3:18 am.

Natalia got out of bed and walked out onto the balcony into the night air. Around and below her the town was dark and still. Not a light shone in any of the windows of the nearby houses. She knew that on the other side of town Umberto and Maria Amadeo slept peacefully, unconcerned that their continuous silence had inflicted such misery on her family. A rage began to build in her.

Inside her room, Natalia dressed quickly. Careful not to wake her children, she quietly made her way downstairs to the front door and stepped out into the street. Propelled by anger and disgust, she walked briskly towards the Amadeo house, not knowing what she intended to do when she reached it. She crossed the deserted piazza, passed her grocery store on the next street, and continued through the shadowed side streets until she could see the house up ahead. In a moment of fury, she began to run and didn't stop until she was standing in the Amadeo's driveway. Looking up at the darkened windows, her breath coming in short bursts, she was surprised to find tears streaming down her cheeks. "Amadeo," she said to herself, "God will punish you for this."

* * *

Luciano sat up in bed watching the small television in his room, a luxury item afforded him as an employee of the Casa. He had spent the day in an angst-ridden fog, mechanically going through the motions of his work. When one of the sisters asked him if he wanted to come in for lunch, he ignored her until she approached him with a worried face and asked if he was all right. Not hungry, he had told her and then went back to his gardening. At the end of the day, he ate a light supper of soup and bread and spent the rest of the night listlessly watching comedies and talk shows. He had not gone for one of his long nighttime walks in the city. He didn't want to think, didn't want to relive the shock he had had that morning, afraid of being crushed by his guilt and sorrow at seeing his son's retreating figure in the garden.

Mindlessly flipping through the channels, Luciano's attention was drawn to the opening scene of a documentary about the immigration museum in New York City. A dark-haired young man—the tour guide and narrator—stood on the deck of a ferry gliding over the dark waters of the Hudson River, a breeze tousling his hair and rippling the fabric of his jacket. Behind him, sunshine glinted off the buildings of the New York skyline. As he spoke to the camera in English, Italian subtitles popped up at the bottom of the screen.

The guide explained the history of Ellis Island as the main port of entry for millions entering the United States at the end of the nineteenth and beginning of the twentieth centuries. Luciano imagined what it must have been like for those early people on that island of imposing buildings, entering a new life so different from the ones they had left.

When the ferry reached the island, the young man disembarked, still talking, and brought his viewers into a building that opened into a massive room called the Great Hall. He described the ordeal faced by those who passed through the various stations of this island—the waiting to be called, the medical examinations, the intense fear of being sent back across the wide and indifferent ocean like a film rewinding.

As the guide led his audience through the various exhibitions, Luciano was struck by one room that displayed personal belongings brought from across the sea—trunks, toys, clothing—each one connected to a life. The room was a repository of memories, links to a world forever gone for those who had left it behind. These and the photos of faces, each one reflecting an emotion frozen in time, depressed Luciano. What had become of their lives and their dreams? Who among them had realized happiness from their sacrifices, and who had died in bitter disappointment? Conjuring up the darkness from his own past, it was no mystery why a place such as this could affect Luciano the way it did, why the experiences of people he had never known and who were long dead could cause him to feel such an overwhelming sense of melancholy.

As the documentary concluded with the guide describing the historical significance of this now-defunct immigration station, Luciano turned the television off, but the images of the faces in the photos stayed with him when he got into bed. Unable to fall asleep, he envisioned the faces of his own wife and children. Fabiano's had taken on small lines around his eyes, and Luciano hoped it was due only to the natural effects of time rather than worry or anxiety. And what about Natalia and Liliana? Had Natalia aged gracefully, or was her beauty marred by the pain he had caused her? These thoughts were not new. They had invaded his conscience many times over the years, yet he always managed to push them away. But now ghosts had come to Rome in the form of Eva Amadeo and his son, and Luciano could no longer ignore what he knew he must do. It was time for him to go home.

Luciano sat up, switched on the bedside lamp, and pulled a sheet of paper and a pen from the nightstand drawer. He was not good with words, and so he grappled with how to tell Sister Michela that he was leaving the Casa di Santa Rosalia. There was so much to say, yet he couldn't bring himself to admit how he had deceived her and the sisters for so long. Every time he started to write the truth, his shame overwhelmed him. In the end, he decided that brevity was best, or at least all that he was capable of. He thanked her for her generosity, asked forgiveness for leaving so abruptly, and explained only that he had found his family. He would miss her and the sisters. Maybe one day, when he had cultivated some courage, he would come back to Rome to see them.

After making his bed for the last time, Luciano packed his clothes and his few possessions in the duffel bag the sisters had given him for Christmas one year—in case he ever wanted to take a short vacation, they had said. They didn't know he would someday use it to run away from them. The intensity of his pain surprised him as he got ready to leave. He placed Sister Michela's letter on the nightstand, switched off the lamp, and, feeling like a gutless thief, left the Casa by the back entrance. Once outside, he headed towards the Roma Termini railway station.

Chapter 17

May 31

Driving through the streets of Rome in the afternoon sunshine, Fabiano glanced at his mother in the passenger seat. He had decided the restless night before that he would return to the Casa di Santa Rosalia the next day and plead with Luciano to return to Benvenuto. He had risen before sunrise intending to sneak out of the house, but Natalia had heard him and insisted on going with him, leaving Liliana to watch the store. Now, seeing his mother's face pale and pinched, he knew that bringing her was a mistake. He did not trust that her reaction to seeing his father would be anything less than volcanic, and he worried what effect that meeting would have on Luciano's decision to return home.

"The guest house is just on the other side of those buildings," he said, pointing his chin ahead.

Natalia nodded slowly but said nothing. She had been silent for most of the long drive.

"Are you sure you're ready for this, mama?"

"I've been ready for a long time, Fabi."

After a few more turns through the streets, Fabiano pulled the car up in front of the Casa and turned the ignition off. Without looking at his mother, he sat quietly, his head bent. "What will you say to him?" he asked.

"I don't know."

"Maybe you should stay in the car and let me go in first."

"I didn't come all this way to wait out here. Let's go."

Natalia got out of the car, and Fabiano followed.

"Don't worry," said Natalia. "I won't make a scene."

There was no one at the reception desk when they entered.

"Wait here," said Fabiano as he headed towards the French doors that led to the garden.

"Where are you going?" she asked. "Wait for someone to come."

"Just wait there," he said over his shoulder.

In the garden a few guests sat on the benches. Some quietly read while others chatted to one another amid the chirping of birds. The signs of Luciano's work—the neat flower beds and trimmed hedges—were all around, but Luciano himself was absent.

When Fabiano returned to the foyer, he found his mother sitting in a chair by the door and the same sister who had admitted him the previous day standing behind the desk. But instead of a bright smile, the sister wore a grave expression. Natalia looked deflated and about to cry.

"Mama, what's going on?"

"You're back," said the sister. "And I understand you're looking for Bruno again."

"Yes, I am. Mama, what did you tell the sister?"

"I simply asked for Bruno." Her voice was flat and low.

"He's not here," said the sister.

"Do you know when he'll be back?"

"He won't be back. He left some time before this morning, I'm told."

"I don't understand."

The sister looked like she, too, wanted to cry. "As I explained to the *signora*, we were told only that he had left and that he had resigned his post here."

Fabiano felt as if someone had punched him in the stomach. "Do you know where we can find him?"

"I'm sorry, but no. He didn't say."

"But surely he must have given some reason for leaving."

"As I said, *signore*, he just left without warning and without a forwarding address. We're all grieved by this. Bruno was a part of our family here, and we're all in somewhat of a shock."

Fabiano turned to his mother. "Let's go," he said.

Natalia seemed unable to get up from the chair.

"Mama, please."

When she still didn't get up, Fabiano thanked the sister, took Natalia by the arm, and led her out to the car. She yielded without a word.

After helping her into the passenger seat, Fabiano got in and together they sat in silence for several minutes before he spoke. "We'll find him, mama. I promise, even if we have to search all of Rome." Fabiano's anger choked his throat so that his words came out clipped.

But Natalia replied in a tone he was not used to hearing from her. It was a tone of total defeat. "No," she said. "Let him be. This is what he wants."

"Mama!"

"Let's go home, Fabi."

"No. He cannot do this a second time. I won't let him get away with it."

Fabiano's voice had risen, and in the closeness of the small car Natalia's expression changed from apathy to distaste. "I want to go home," she said.

"That's it? You're giving up?"

Natalia sighed wearily. "What do you want me to do, track down a man who clearly does not want to be found?"

"Mama," he said, carefully measuring his words, "I have done everything you have asked of me. I flew three thousand miles to confront a woman who turned out not to be keeping house with your husband. I have been to Rome twice in two days to find that husband, and I have driven nearly six hours today to get here, and now you tell me to turn around and drive back without even attempting to look for him. Is this fair?"

"We can spend the day here if you don't want to drive. We can get rooms at a hotel this evening. But tomorrow morning I want to leave. There's no point in being here."

Fabiano slammed his palm on the steering wheel. He sat back for a few moments, unable to look at his mother, then started the ignition. "We're going home now," he said bitterly, driving off.

* * *

It was late afternoon by the time Luciano, after making three train connections, stepped onto the platform at Santa Chiara. Across the tracks and far in the distance, the sea glided gently up and back upon the shore. He was really here now, about to walk back into his past.

Luciano hurried past the taxi stand at the bottom of the platform. While waiting in the Termini the night before, he had decided he would not take a taxi into Benvenuto. After so long a time, his entry would have to be inconspicuous. No one should see him before he had time to meet with his family. No one should deliver the message that he was back in town except him. He owed Natalia and his children that much. He would walk up the mountain.

Stepping into the street, Luciano looked around to see if he recognized anyone walking. The train station was in the center of town. Would anyone recognize *him* from the countless times he had come to the shore on market days, to the supermarket and the other stores and places of business in the town? He had aged, but not that much. And what would he say if anyone approached him? He was sure the people of Santa Chiara had heard of his disappearance all those years ago. There was no keeping secrets for miles around in this part of the world. Maybe they had forgotten about it. Maybe Luciano Benini was not so important that people would remember his face.

Luciano walked briskly. To his relief, he didn't recognize the few people he passed. One woman looked familiar, but she paid him no attention. He looked for signs of change since he had last been there but could find none, other than an occasional improvement to the buildings that had been there for generations—a new coat of paint, a new awning, an updated street sign. The supermarket that had been his destination on the day of the feast was still there. He slowed as he passed it, stopping to look as one who gawks with macabre curiosity upon some place of deadly disaster. A chill shook him. That was where it had all begun, the first link in a chain of events that would ultimately bring him back full circle.

A few blocks from the supermarket, the main road wound up the mountain. There he ran a greater risk of meeting someone from Benvenuto driving either to or from the town, but this could not be avoided.

Luciano reached the road and began the long walk home. There was not a lot of traffic, but whenever a car passed, he turned his face away. His legs ached. He was not used to the steep incline of the mountain as he had been in earlier days. Several times he stopped to catch his breath. He continued in this way until he reached the road that branched off to Benvenuto and turned onto it.

Memories rushed through him as he walked towards the town. He knew it would have changed little, as few of these ancient towns did, and in his mind he followed the familiar streets, passing houses, shops, *his* shop, the church, and the piazza, until in his imagination he saw the front door of his house where his wife and daughter waited. Only they didn't know they waited. They didn't know he was about to unexpectedly crash into their world. He wondered what Fabiano had told them, and if he would be greeted with a welcome or a door slammed in his face.

As Benvenuto came into view, Luciano left the road and headed into the countryside.

* * *

When Fabiano parked the car in front of the Benini house and got out, Natalia made no move to follow. When he opened the passenger side door and took her arm to help her, she moved mechanically, limply, like an old woman.

As it was early evening, Liliana was home from the shop when they entered the foyer.

"What happened?" she asked, looking past them. "Didn't he come with you?"

Natalia released Fabiano's arm and began to slowly walk up the stairs. "He was not there," she said flatly, as if commenting on the weather, and continued her way up as Liliana fired anxious questions at Fabiano.

Once in her bedroom, the door closed and the agitated talk of her children muffled, Natalia undressed and got into bed. She had a headache, and every bone in her body hurt. She had no desire even to confront Umberto Amadeo. She had no desire for anything. For the second time in her life, Natalia was in mourning for the same man. Curling her arms around her pillow, she closed her eyes and silently prayed for sleep.

* * *

The sun was dipping behind the mountain when Luciano returned to the spot where he had last encountered Eva Amadeo. He had spent hours walking around the countryside, stopping now and then to sit on the grass and take in the geography of his earlier life. Everywhere he looked, scenes that had been tucked away in his memory stood vividly alive before him: the olive groves and vineyards, the network of curving roads, the farmers' houses standing alone on vast patches of land. He had passed the cemetery where his own parents were buried and looked in through the closed gates at the stone slabs topped with crosses and headstones. At different points in his rambling, he could see Benvenuto in the distance, and the sight of it both thrilled and frightened him. When occasionally he saw someone walking in the distance, it was easy to find a secluded spot among the trees and rocks where he could remain unseen. And now here he was, sitting on the same flat boulder where Eva had sat crying all those years before.

Luciano tried to remember which of the trees he had clung to before falling, but after so many years they all looked the same. Looking down into the ravine, he imagined his body lying there, unconscious, and how it must have looked to Eva Amadeo. What had she been thinking, seeing him there, unmoving? Maybe she thought he was dead. And what had she done immediately after? If he had not harmed her as he feared, then she was fully capable of running back to town to tell everyone that Luciano Benini was at the bottom of a ravine. If she had done that, they would have come looking for him, and he would not have awakened alone and broken with pain in the moonlight. So why had she not alerted anyone?

Luciano struggled to make sense of what had occurred that night, recalling the sound of the fireworks, the pain in his body as he fell, hitting against the trees and shrubs on his way down. Realizing he might never know the answers to all his questions, he looked up to find that the sky had darkened. He sat for a few moments more before getting to his feet. It was time to go into town and face his wife and daughter.

Stepping onto the dirt path that led back to the road, he saw a man walking towards him against the faint glow of sunset outlining the mountain. Luciano did not try to avoid him. He could not have done so even if he wanted to because the man was walking directly towards him, and Luciano knew he had been seen. The man's steps quickened as he got closer. It was Father Pietro.

The father's shocked expression froze Luciano, and for a moment neither one spoke or moved. Then the priest stepped forward and embraced him—he, the prodigal son returned home—and gratitude welled up in Luciano.

"I don't believe it," said Father Pietro, releasing him. "There was talk that Luciano Benini had been found, but you know how people gossip. And now you're really here."

Luciano nodded and smiled. "Yes, here I am."

"But what are you doing out here, Luciano? Why are you not at home with your family?"

"I'm on my way there. What are you doing out here, father? Still taking your nightly walks? That's one thing you and I have in common."

Father Pietro's expression became solemn. "What happened to you, Luciano? Where have you been all these years?"

Luciano sighed deeply. "There's no quick answer to that, I'm afraid."

"I don't suspect there is." Father Pietro shook his head and smiled. "I still can't believe you're here standing in front of me." He took Luciano by the arm, and together they walked towards the town.

* * *

Fabiano sat stiffly in his mother's kitchen, his phone in hand. Every time he thought he had enough control over his emotions to confront Eva Amadeo, a new wave of anger prevented him from calling her. He and Liliana had not seen or heard from their mother since she had secluded herself in her bedroom hours before. When Liliana opened the bedroom door to check on her, Natalia appeared to be asleep, but Fabiano suspected she was faking it so that she would not be disturbed. How could she sleep after all she had been through?

"Are you going to call her or not?" asked Liliana, placing a glass of wine on the table in front of Fabiano. She poured one for herself and sat down across from him. "If you're not going to, I'll call her myself." She tried to take the phone from him, but Fabiano resisted.

"I'll do it," he said. He tapped the number in his phone and waited for Eva to answer. She was probably at the café now, as it was late afternoon in New York.

Eva's voice on the other end sounded cautious. "Hello?"

"It's Fabiano," he said softly.

"Fabiano," she said, her voice brightening. "I wasn't sure who was calling. You didn't give me your number."

"You didn't ask for it."

"I was wondering what happened after you left here. Did you find your father?"

"I did."

"So . . . What happened?"

"Why didn't you tell me you were with him the night he disappeared?"

There was silence on the other end.

"You knew what happened to him. You watched as everyone in the town went out looking for him, acting like you knew nothing, when all the while you knew exactly what happened. You let us all wonder and suffer. You let my mother suffer. You—"

"I'm sorry," she blurted. "I didn't mean to. I was terrified."

Liliana pulled at his arm. "What is she saying?"

Fabiano pulled away and ignored her. His attention was on Eva, whose struggle to answer gave him grim satisfaction.

"I saw him fall," Eva continued. "I thought he was dead."

"And you thought it was okay to keep that to yourself?"

"I thought I had killed him. I didn't know what to do, so I ran home, and when I went back with my father, he was gone."

"Your father? So he knew, too."

"He was trying to protect me."

"By allowing *my* father to crawl off into the woods to die like a wounded animal?"

"We thought he would be found. And if he weren't dead, if he was just hurt, he would come home."

"But he didn't, did he? You lied to the police. I'll make sure they know about this."

"I *am* sorry, Fabiano. So very, very sorry."

The remorse in her voice was so real that Fabiano almost felt sorry for her. Almost. "The only reason," he said, "why I'm not at your father's house right now is because I'm afraid that if I see him, I will kill him."

Eva's voice trembled. "It's not his fault. He was only looking out for me."

Fabiano did not wait to hear any more of Eva's pleas. He cut off the conversation and threw the phone across the table.

"Tell me," said Liliana. "Tell me what she said."

Fabiano recounted the conversation to Liliana, who sat listening with her wine glass clutched between her fingers. "What are you going to do now?" she asked. "You're not going to confront Umberto tonight, are you?"

"Didn't you hear what I just told her?"

Liliana pushed Fabiano's wine glass closer to him. "Take some. You need to relax."

Fabiano drank the wine in a few gulps and sat back, listless and feeling as if he were made of wax.

"Go tomorrow," said Liliana. "I'll go with you. He needs to account for what he did."

Fabiano snorted. "What good will it do?"

"You can't let him get away with this."

After a long pause, Fabiano took a deep breath. "Tomorrow I'll go to the police. I doubt they'll do anything after all this time, but at least I can make a formal complaint. I'll insist that they question him, if nothing else. Give him something to worry about. And as soon as I'm finished, I'm going back to Florence."

"But what about Umberto?"

"Let the police handle him. I have a job to go back to."

Fabiano kissed his sister on the cheek and went upstairs to bed.

* * *

Eva needed air. Her office at the Crystal Café seemed smaller than usual, the walls close and tight around her. She felt light-headed and struggled to keep from breaking down in tears. Without telling the staff, she left the Crystal and walked slowly home.

Living in America, Eva was not afraid of the Italian police. And she was sure they would not bother themselves with opening an old case, so her family in Benvenuto was safe. It was not fear, then, that choked her but her long-buried shame of having lied to the police, depriving the Beninis of a starting point in their search for Luciano. When she had told Fabiano that his father was in Rome, she hadn't considered that Luciano would recall her part in the accident and tell his son. She had thought only of reuniting them.

Eva reached her house and was greeted by Marcus Aurelius jumping on her as she entered the foyer. "Not now," she said, stroking the dog's head.

Marcus followed her into the living room where she threw herself onto the sofa. She might never know exactly what had happened to Luciano after his fall or why he had denied knowing her and knowing Benvenuto, but none of that concerned her anymore. She had to make things right.

Eva pulled her phone from her pocket and called her father. After several rings, the phone went to voicemail. "It's me, papa. I need to talk to you. Fabiano Benini knows I was with Luciano that night. Call me."

Eva hung up and called Stella. "I don't know what to do," she said. "I don't know how to fix this."

"Fix what? What happened?"

"Fabiano Benini knows I was with his father the night he fell."

"So? Wait . . . how do you know this?"

Eva recounted her phone conversation with Fabiano.

"So what are you so upset about?" asked Stella.

"What do you mean? My lies cost that family fifteen years of heartache."

"You had no choice."

"Of course I did."

"Eva, you were a terrified teenage girl. You told your parents. It's not like you kept it completely to yourself."

"And they covered it up."

"Yes. So stop beating yourself up over it."

"It wasn't right."

"Maybe not, but that's the way it happened."

Eva felt drained. All she wanted was to curl up in bed and shut out the events of the past three weeks, pretending they had never happened. "What am I going to do, Stella?"

"You're going to forget about it, that's what."

Eva's call waiting started to beep. "I need to go. My father is trying to reach me."

"Okay, but stop—"

Eva didn't wait for Stella to finish before switching over to her father. "Papa," she said, "Fabiano Benini has threatened to call the police on you—on us—for saying we didn't know anything about Luciano's disappearance."

"So? Do you really think they'll do anything about this now?"

"No, I don't. I'm not worried about the police. I'm worried about the Beninis coming after you."

"I can handle the Beninis."

"But they have a right to be angry, papa. If I had told the truth all those years ago, they might have found Luciano sooner."

"Sooner than what? There were search parties, Eva. No one could find him. Wherever he managed to go, a few hours would have made no difference. This was a man who did not want to be found."

"I wish I could believe that."

"You told me that when you saw him, he denied knowing anything at all about Benvenuto. Yet he told his son you were with him the night of the feast. Do you not see a contradiction here?"

Eva struggled to find some comfort in what her father was saying. He was right, of course. Luciano had stayed away of his own volition. But if only she had acted differently, he might not have had time to run off. If he had been found sooner, he might have thought twice about leaving.

"Eva?"

"I want to come home, papa. I want to sort this out with the Beninis."

"Don't be ridiculous! What could you possibly say that would make any difference to them? They hate us."

"I can ask for forgiveness. I can ask how to make it up to them."

"And they will throw you out. Eva, there have been feuds going on in these little towns for generations. There's nothing you can do. Just let it be."

Eva hung up with a promise to her father that she would put this all behind her. As she put the phone down, Marcus Aurelius nudged up against her. She was calmer now. Stroking the dog's fur soothed her, and her father's words had helped ease her conscience. He was right, as usual. She was ready to take whatever punishment the Beninis had to give her, but she knew, also, that they wouldn't listen to her no matter how much she pleaded for forgiveness. Not now, anyway. One day she would figure out how to make amends. But until then, she would no longer allow guilt and regret to taint her life like a stain on her soul. Luciano was alive and delivered back to his family. That was all that mattered.

Eva led Marcus to the foyer and attached his leash to his collar. "Just a short walk," she said to the dog, who looked up at her with liquid eyes, his tail wagging furiously. "And then I have to get back to work. The staff must be wondering where I am."

Chapter 18

Luciano had forgotten how much he liked Father Pietro. The priest was a true man of God, kind of heart and humble in demeanor. He remembered the night Natalia had humiliated him when he had accidentally thrown up on the father's shoes. Father Pietro had not gotten angry and had tried to calm Natalia down as she shouted. Now, walking along with him in the quiet of the night, Luciano felt the same kind of peace he often felt in his garden at the Casa di Santa Rosalia. For a moment, the thought of that garden sent a wave of sadness over him.

They strolled silently towards the town under the black night sky. As they got closer, the lights of Benvenuto—the amber glow of windows, the streetlamps casting dim pools on the streets —struck Luciano with a nostalgic blow. The nearness of this place, the reality that he would be walking its streets again and entering his house, made him stop.

Father Pietro placed a hand on his shoulder. "I'm sure this isn't easy for you," he said.

"What if they don't want me? My family, I mean."

"Luciano, your wife sent your son to America to find you. Why would they not want you?"

Luciano was deeply puzzled. "She sent him to America?"

"You didn't know?"

"No. He never mentioned that. Why would she send him to America?"

"You'd better let Natalia explain that."

"Fabiano came to see me in Rome, and I sent him away. I'm a terrible person, father."

"You may have done terrible things, but you can make up for them."

"How? How do I make up for abandoning my family?"

"You'll find a way."

"It wasn't intentional, not at first anyway."

"You don't have to explain anything to me unless you want to."

"I need confession, father. All those years I spent at a convent guest house, I never went to Mass. I never felt worthy. There's so much I regret."

"When you're ready, come to me and confess all you need to. God is forgiving."

"I want to do it now."

"It can wait until tomorrow."

"No. I'm afraid my shame will kill me, father. How can I face them? At least if God forgives me, I can go in there with some dignity."

Father Pietro nodded. "Okay," he said.

Luciano breathed deeply and looked up at the stars. "It's been a long time, twenty years at least since my last confession."

"I can walk you through it."

Standing on the side of the road, guided by Father Pietro's prompting questions, Luciano's deepest regrets poured from his lips and dissipated in the night air. By the time he was finished and received the blessing that absolved him of his sins, Luciano's anxiety had lifted.

"Say three Our Fathers and two Hail Marys as your penance," said Father Pietro. "Say them now. I'll wait."

As Father Pietro walked away from him, Luciano protested. "That's it? For everything I've done all I get is three Our Fathers and two Hail Marys?"

"Yes. Now say them so we can be on our way."

Luciano turned from the priest and began to pray. It was hard at first. It had been so long since he had done this, but the familiar prayers, memorized in childhood, were deep in his soul, and as he said them a wrenching in his chest loosened the words out of him.

The prayers finished, Luciano went to Father Pietro's side. "Let's go, father."

The road they were on led directly into the main street of Benvenuto. Passing the dark, empty shops, only the glow of the streetlamps lit the way for Luciano and Father Pietro. Luciano forgot how still the nights in a mountain town could be.

They turned off into a side alley and wound their way through the maze of narrow streets towards the Benini house.

"You remember your way," said Father Pietro.

"This was my home."

"Is. This *is* your home." Father Pietro looked at him sideways. "You are staying, aren't you?"

Luciano sighed and shrugged. "That all depends on Natalia. If she accepts me, then certainly I'll stay."

"She will."

"How can you be so sure?"

"Believe me, Luciano. That woman never got over losing you. Natalia may have her faults, like all of us do, but she's a good woman. She's remained loyal to you all these years."

Father Pietro looked at him sideways again, asking the unspoken question with a raising of his eyebrows.

"Well, you may not believe this," said Luciano, "but there have been no other women for me, either. Not in all these years."

The father smiled. "I do believe you."

The two men rounded a corner, and both instinctively stopped. Down the street, Luciano's house was quietly closed up, its windows shuttered except for one upstairs that was open to the air, although the room within was dark. This was Liliana's bedroom. Struck with nervous anticipation, Luciano waited to see if the light would go on, if his daughter would appear at the window to close it, but moments passed, and no one came. Downstairs at street level, the front door looked heavy and forbidding.

"Come on," urged Father Pietro, taking Luciano by the arm.

"I can't, father." Luciano's fear rooted him to the street so that the priest's pulling on his arm did no good. "I need more time."

"You've had fifteen years." Father Pietro's tone was firm.

"What will I say to them?"

"Look, I know this is difficult, but you've come this far."

Father Pietro tugged at Luciano's arm, leading him forward, and this time Luciano did not resist. They reached the house and Father Pietro turned to go.

"Good luck, Luciano. I'll come by tomorrow to see how you are."

"Can't you stay? At least until I see what kind of reception I get?"

Father Pietro nodded.

Taking a deep breath, Luciano rang the doorbell. A few moments later, approaching footsteps sounded in the foyer.

"Who's there?"

Even after all this time Luciano recognized his daughter's voice. A sharp pain pierced his chest. He didn't know what to say.

"Liliana," said Father Pietro through the door. "There's someone here to see you."

The door opened, and as Fabiano came out of the kitchen to see who had rung the bell, Liliana stood staring at her father, her mouth agape.

* * *

Natalia, deep in her indifference and unable to sleep, paid little attention to the buzz of the doorbell even at so late an hour. But when Fabiano's voice came up excitedly from the foyer, she sat up in bed and strained to hear. If it was Amadeo come to give them more grief, she would go downstairs and throw him out.

Natalia got out of bed and reached for the pink satin robe that lay thrown across the chair by her dresser. Barefoot and ready to defend her family, she opened her bedroom door to the sound of a commotion that had now migrated to the living room. Among the excited voices one stood out, familiar yet impossible. Natalia rushed down the stairs.

All conversation stopped as Natalia entered the living room. Before her, in the center of the room, stood four people. Her son, whose face, strangely, looked both apprehensive and elated, had his arm around his sister, who seemed mystified by the situation she found herself in. The priest was there, Father Pietro, looking expectant and hopeful, but what caused Natalia to catch her breath, what pinned her feet to the carpet, was the sight of the man standing beside him.

Natalia's legs gave out. She was saved from collapsing to the floor by the priest and Fabiano rushing to help her over to the sofa. She did not take her gaze from her husband, who seemed incapable of coming near her.

Liliana came and sat beside her. Pulling her mother's hands onto her lap and gently squeezing them, she said nothing, her eyes wide.

It was the priest who spoke first. "Get something for your mother, Fabiano. A glass of water or maybe something stronger."

Fabiano went to the credenza and pulled out a bottle of grappa, poured a small glass for his mother, and gave it to her. Natalia pushed the glass away.

The room was still. It seemed nobody knew what to say to her, how to react to her presence there. They watched her watch her husband, who had not moved from where he stood since she had first entered.

"Mama," said Fabiano gently, "please say something."

A haze enveloped Natalia's mind but her eyes were clear. They saw Luciano in sharp relief against the backdrop of their home, the home the two of them had shared and in which they had raised their children. Like a film rapidly rolling, Natalia saw in her imagination the details of their life together—the day of their wedding and joyfully coming to this house after the reception; the late-night conversations in the early years of their marriage curled up on the sofa; bringing Fabiano home from the hospital; Liliana's first steps; and the later years, the arguments and the reconciliations; the criticisms they threw at one another; the remorse and the apologies; the normal trials and misadventures of a marriage in which they both engaged—and something in her brain awakened and she became the Natalia that Benvenuto knew, the Natalia that always spoke her mind and never ran from adversity. She stared at her husband with an intensity that caused Luciano visible agitation. He shifted his gaze to the wall and back again, clasping his hands and pursing his lips. Twice his mouth moved as if to say something, then rapidly shut.

"Why must I say something?" said Natalia quietly. "Why must I be the one?"

At the sound of her voice, a change came over Luciano. He took a step forward and looked squarely at her without reticence.

Waiting for him to speak, Natalia stared into his face defiantly, a face that had changed little in the past decade and a half. It was fuller now, his eyes framed with deeper lines, and his hair was grayer, but the Luciano she knew was still very much there.

"Natalia . . ." The muscles in Luciano's face tightened as he struggled to address her.

Natalia saw remorse there, but it did nothing to ease her anger and pain. She continued to stare at him, unwilling to question him, unwilling to help him find the words.

"We should leave them alone," said Father Pietro to Fabiano and Liliana.

"No," said Luciano, "they need to hear this."

"Then I will go," said the priest.

Luciano looked nervous, as if Father Pietro's presence provided a shield for him against anything unpleasant that might follow, and for a moment Natalia pitied him. But Luciano did not protest.

"Thank you, father. Thank you for getting me this far."

Father Pietro clasped him on the shoulder and said his goodbyes to the family. "You all know where to find me if you need me."

When Liliana left her mother's side to walk the priest to the door, Luciano took her place on the sofa. "I know I have a lot to answer for," he said, "and I honestly don't know where to begin."

The sound of a closing door was heard in the foyer, and a moment later Liliana returned. She went to Fabiano, who had remained standing by the sofa, her demeanor meek and uncertain. Natalia turned to both of them. "Go upstairs," she said. "I want to talk to your father alone."

Liliana looked stricken. "But mama . . ."

"Please, Liliana."

Fabiano took his sister by the arm. "Leave them alone for now," he said. "Let's give them some privacy."

Passing her father on the way out of the room, Liliana broke from Fabiano, threw her arms around Luciano, and hugged him tightly. It was a sudden and swift move, over before Luciano could react.

After her children had left the room, Natalia turned again to her husband with a hard look. "So," she said, "do you want to tell me why you abandoned us?"

Luciano licked his lips. His mouth had become a desert. "It wasn't supposed to turn out that way," he said.

"But it did, and if you don't start explaining, I'm going to throw you out on the street, and this time you can stay away for good."

Luciano recounted how he had wandered out into the countryside on the night of the feast, admitting that he had been drunk, and come across Eva, whose crying had reminded him so much of Liliana at that moment, so young and vulnerable, that he only wanted to help her. He described all he could remember about his fall into the ravine and losing consciousness.

"I couldn't find my way out of there, Natalia. I kept blacking out. I would've come home that night but physically I was not able to."

"Why were you drunk? Where did you go after you left the house that afternoon? You didn't go to the feast."

"No, I went to the shop, into the back room. I was tired of arguing with you and wanted to be alone. I had more to drink and . . ."

"And what?"

"And then I went for a walk, like I told you. I didn't expect to see Eva out there."

As Luciano recounted the events that followed his fall, Natalia paid attention to the cadence of his voice and watched his expressions change: surprise as he described awakening to find Eva's bloody shawl; apprehensive as he told of fleeing the hospital and lying his way into a job at the convent guest house; guilt and pain as he recounted how his decision to remain in Rome for a short time had stretched into years until he was too ashamed to come back to Benvenuto. His face was like a canvas of moving brush strokes, the artist painting and re-painting every line and curve until finally deciding on a portrait of remorse.

When he had finished, Luciano tried to take Natalia's hand, but she pulled it away. "I won't blame you," he said, "if you tell me to leave and never enter this house again, but I hope and pray that you don't."

His story was hardly believable. It was too fantastic, like the plot of a bad film, yet Natalia knew it was true. She could always tell when Luciano was trying to hide the truth, like when he made up excuses for why he was not home on time for dinner, or where he was when he was supposed to be at the store but instead left Liliana to mind the customers while he wandered off. She could not believe that he was with her now, sitting beside her. Yet there he was, asking for her forgiveness. Her anger remained but it began to weaken. Natalia imagined it as a ball of wax sitting deep in her chest, still solid, but softening, its outer layer melting. "Do you know," she said, "that I sent Fabiano to America to look for you?"

Luciano's brow creased. "Father Pietro told me. But why?"

"Because I thought you had run off with Eva all those years ago."

To her irritation, Luciano let out a short bark of laughter. "Why would you think that?"

"Never mind that," she said sharply. "Do you know how much pain you have caused this family? How much distress?"

Luciano stared down at his hands clasped in his lap.

"I don't know what to do with you, Luciano."

Natalia got up and walked to the credenza where Fabiano had left the glass of grappa he had poured for her earlier. She drank the liquor with slow sips. When she had finished, she came back to the sofa and stood over Luciano, who looked up at her meekly.

"You have a lot to make up for," she said.

"I know. But if you'll only—"

"You will have to prove yourself to this family if we're to ever trust you again."

Luciano raised his eyebrows. "So then—"

"Believe me, I don't intend to make it easy for you."

"Anything," he said, "anything you want to do is fine with me."

"You can sleep down here tonight. And when Fabiano goes back to Florence, you can take his room."

"Natalia, thank you, my love. I promise I'll—"

Natalia put up her hand. "I don't want to hear any promises."

"I understand. You need more than words."

"Exactly. And now I'm going to bed."

She turned out the light as she left the room, leaving Luciano sitting in the dark.

* * *

Fabiano, his bedroom door slightly ajar, heard his mother coming up the stairs. He knew her step, and although he did not expect his father to come upstairs with her, still he was disappointed. Out of respect for their mother's privacy, both he and Liliana had resisted the temptation to eavesdrop on their parents' conversation. Instead, Fabiano went to bed and attempted to sleep, but his mind was restless going over the day's events, wondering how the night would end for his parents.

A slice of light from the hallway widened into the room as Natalia poked her head in. Fabiano sat up in bed. "Is everything all right?" he asked.

"Yes, I think so."

"Where's papa?"

"Downstairs. Good night."

"Is he staying?"

"He's back now. We may as well keep him."

As Natalia closed the door, Fabiano smiled. He waited to hear his mother's door close before getting out of bed and going to his sister's room.

Liliana opened her door to his knock. "I can't sleep," she said in a low voice. "Do you know what happened?"

"He's staying."

Liliana's eyes widened. "Is he in there with her?" she whispered, pointing across the hall at her mother's room.

"No, not yet. I suspect she'll make him wait a long time."

"Let's go down and talk to him."

"I think there's been enough talk for today. Let him rest." Fabiano kissed his sister goodnight and went back to bed.

Lying awake in the moonlight filtering through his half-shuttered window, Fabiano reflected on how his movements of the past couple of weeks—traveling from Florence to Benvenuto to New York to Rome and back to Benvenuto—had exhausted him physically and mentally, but most of all emotionally. He was grateful that his long-lost father was home, that Luciano had come back showing true repentance. Now his mother's pain could begin to heal.

As he considered all that had happened, including the role the Amadeos had played in this drama, his anger towards them softened. In many ways, Eva, too, had been a victim of circumstance that night of the feast. She was still just a girl at the time, and while she should have come forward, it was not her fault, nor her father's, that Luciano had chosen to stay away all these years. And in the end, it was the Amadeos, after all, who had helped them find Luciano.

Fabiano's muscles, tense for most of the day, loosened, and a welcome drowsiness came over him. Tomorrow he would call the university and ask for a few more days' leave. He missed his adopted city, with its elegant beauty and ancient artistic spirit, but his return there could wait now that he had a father to get reacquainted with.

And tomorrow he would call Eva Amadeo. He would tell her that there would be no police report. He would tell her the details of what had happened to Luciano, if she cared to hear them, and he would ask if maybe the next time she was in Benvenuto they could meet for coffee or a glass of wine.

Fabiano turned on his side to face the window. Through the opening in the shutters, the roofs of the town were dark against the black outline of the mountain. Nothing moved in the streets of Benvenuto except the breeze.

About the Author

Lisa Sita is a native and resident of Queens, New York, where she writes in various genres, teaches anthropology, and serves as an academic advisor to ESL students at the City University of New York. Her professional background includes work as a museum educator, curriculum writer, and author of educational books for young readers. Lisa holds a Master of Fine Arts in Writing and a Bachelor of Arts and a Master of Arts in Anthropology. Visit her website at lisasita.com.

www.ingramcontent.com/pod-product-compliance
Lightning Source LLC
Chambersburg PA
CBHW060604190726
48283CB00003B/1152